He started to put the gun in Julie's hand to get her fingerprints on it and checked himself. Hadn't he read something about tests for powder marks to show if a person had fired a gun—paraffin tests or whatever they were?

Or had he read something else that said they weren't reliable?

Well, Julie's hand had better show them, just as a precaution.

It was an awkward business to position her hand on the gun, finger on the trigger, and risky, too, in case the sound of the shot brought her out of her stupor. He steadied her arm and aimed at the sofa, pulling the trigger with his finger over hers exerting her pressure.

Julie moaned but didn't come to. He placed the gun on the floor beside her chair to look as if she had dropped it. Her glass came next, his prints wiped off, hers pressed on as with the gun.

Claude's glance settled on Julie, the patsy, the sitting duck . . .

No one would hold Alix's death against her—because who could say what they'd do themselves if they were dead drunk? It could almost be looked at like a drunken driver killing someone on the highway.

Even for himself, it could be looked at like that. God knew, he hadn't meant to kill Alix. It was the things she had said . . .

THREE'S A CROWD

DORIS MILES DISNEY
THREE'S A CROWD

ZEBRA BOOKS
KENSINGTON PUBLISHING CORP.

ZEBRA BOOKS

are published by

Kensington Publishing Corp.
475 Park Avenue South
New York, NY 10016

First printing: May 1987

Printed in the United States of America

For Laura Unterspan
Half-star general, five-star friend

1

"Julie's abortion was before my time, of course," Claude Whitfield said. "I didn't even meet Alix until almost two years later. But God knows"—he shook his head—"I've heard so much about it there are times when I feel I must have performed it myself."

Emily Bartlett smiled hesitantly. She said nothing.

He put his own interpretation on the smile and added, "Don't know why I'm burdening you with the Dunham family history, Emily. We're supposed to be talking business, aren't we? Trouble is"—he gave her an apologetic grin—"you're too good a listener."

"Am I? That's not much of a compliment. Makes me seem mousy." There was no hesitancy in her smile this time. She was gently teasing him.

She had a nice smile, he thought. A nice face. Not beautiful. Not at all like Alix who was considered a real beauty with her classic features, exquisitely fair complexion, and gilt hair. But a nice face just the same with warm brown eyes, lovely expressive eyes that reflected her amusement as she smiled at him. Attractive, nothing more than that, was the word to describe her looks. He had thought her too plain at

7

first but had since changed his mind.

How old was she? Not much past thirty. She didn't even look that but from things she had said about taking an extra semester to finish college because she had switched her major to math, not getting married for over a year after she was graduated and then working with her husband to build up their business, she must be past thirty.

He was forty-five himself. A widow in her early thirties was just right for him. Particularly, one without inconvenient family ties here in Northern Virginia.

The waiter hovered with a coffeepot. At Emily's nod he refilled her cup, went around the table to refill Claude's and then melted away.

Emily looked at her watch. "Might as well have my eight o'clock cancer stick early with my coffee," she said.

"What a way to put it," he protested taking out his cigarette case.

"Just a reminder to keep cutting down."

"Slow torture. You have to quit cold or forget it."

She gave an exaggerated sigh. "No willpower, that's me."

Claude Whitfield hoped that her lack of it carried over into areas other than smoking. Bed was what he had in mind. Oh, not right away, considering the hint of reserve in her manner. But later.

He flicked his lighter, held it to her cigarette, lit one himself.

She blew out smoke and said, "Your sister-in-law — Julie, is it? — sounds rather complex, Mr. Whitfield."

"Claude," he corrected her. "I thought you agreed

that we use first names. Yes, Julie surely is. Wild child in her teens, three marriages, two divorces and now the third husband, an upright Connecticut Yankee, seems to have walked out on her. So she lands on us tomorrow. That's part of her life story. She and Alix don't get along at all but she still comes running home when the going gets rough for big sister to help pick up the pieces."

"Will she stay long?"

"Depends on whether her husband will take her back, I reckon. Or how soon she gets bored with Rockwell. For all that it's not too far from Washington, it's still a rather slow-moving Southern town. Certainly different from Greenwich, Connecticut, where Julie's been living. That's more or less a suburb of New York."

"But she was born and raised in Rockwell, she and your wife, too, weren't they?"

"Oh yes. They go back three generations there to Great-granddad Dunham. He started the sawmill that grew into today's office furniture company. My father-in-law, though, was the one who made it a real quality name in the field; enough so to put him in on the ground floor when the big boom came with World War II. Now that he's gone"—Claude adopted a modest note—"I try to keep things moving the way he did."

Emily, with thought of tar and nicotine concentrations, stubbed out her half-smoked cigarette and said, "Seems to me you're doing that, making plans to expand into computer enclosures."

"If it works out," Claude said on the same modest note. "Don't forget Alix's Uncle Paul. He always wants to have his say and he's a real conservative type."

There was also Alix herself to be considered, Emily reflected. Was she as conservative as her uncle — and, more to the point, how much control did she exercise over the company?

Claude answered her unspoken question with his next statement. "Of course Paul doesn't have the deciding vote," he said. "You might call it mine since Alix leaves the running of the business to me. It's not her cup of tea at all."

But even as he said this, Claude played it back in his mind and made a quick revision, establishing a line of retreat in case he couldn't win Alix's approval of his plans that were surefire, he felt himself, and that should bring him new status at Dunham's and a long-overdue raise in salary.

He added hurriedly: "Not that I'd want to force the issue against Paul's judgment. My father-in-law brought him into the company right out of college and he's been there ever since. It wouldn't do for me to start a family feud over something like this. So you see . . ." Claude shrugged and sat back, satisfied that he had covered himself as well as he could if Alix turned him down.

"Yes, I see what you mean." Emily kept her tone neutral as she felt she should while they were still in the preliminary stages of whether or not her firm would be doing business with Dunham's. She set her coffee cup down and said, "This has been very pleasant, Mr. Whitfield, but I really must get home now."

"It's Claude, not mister," he reminded her again.

She smiled. "I just keep forgetting, don't I?"

She wondered if he realized that this was intentional on her part. Working on her own in a man's world had led to a few episodes that made her wary of being too friendly with business associates. But Claude Whitfield's insistence on first names was giving her no choice.

"Well, you can make up for it by having a cordial with me before we leave." He looked around for their waiter. "What would you like?"

"A Cointreau."

Emily studied him while he gave their order. She couldn't remember when, if ever, she'd met a man as handsome as he was. Dramatically so, she thought, with his prematurely white hair—no, not really white, more of a silvery gray—a thick shining crop of it combed to one side, a little longer, probably, than he had worn it two or three years ago. Very dark brows and vivid blue eyes made an arresting contrast to that silver hair. His deep golfer's tan added to the effect.

He had everything going for him, she thought, as her assessment continued. Good bones, broad-shouldered height, an open expression, a youthful, spontaneous smile.

He carried his looks well too. He must know how stunning he was—women fell for him in droves, surely, to judge by the feminine glances he had been attracting all during dinner—but he showed no awareness of them. Not once had his attention strayed from Emily.

He was almost too good to be true.

Whatever he was, though, direct and honest or deep and subtle, was no concern of hers. He was a married man, his wife's employee, regardless of his title of president and her lack of interest in how he ran the company.

But there was his sister-in-law, too, Emily thought next. Didn't Julie, who was arriving in Rockwell tomorrow, own some part of Dunham's?

Her Cointreau was set in front of her. She was pleased, in spite of herself, that Claude Whitfield wanted to prolong their social interlude.

She could ask about Julie. If Bartlett's Computer-Electronic Equipment Distributors was to do business with Dunham's, she might need to know how many voices could be raised in that family-owned corporation.

She took a sip of her cordial and asked, "Doesn't Julie own some part of the company?"

"Julie? Oh yes. She and Alix have an equal interest but Julie has no say in it . . ."

Claude's glance settled on his glass. He turned it between his fingers and said, "Let me tell you a little more about Julie. There was her abortion—I was giving away no secret when I mentioned it earlier because she broadcasts it far and wide herself—at the age of seventeen when she was in boarding school. There was her first marriage, an elopement, at nineteen. That ended two or three years later, not long after Alix and I were married. The divorce created something of a scandal—she was caught in a hotel room with another man—that caused the family a lot of embarrassment, especially my father-in-law who thought Julie was the greatest thing that ever happened. She came home then for a few months but he let her go back to New York. She was drinking quite a bit by that time which didn't help any."

Claude took a sip of his brandy and continued in the same objective tone: "Alix has always felt that the heart attack he had shortly afterward was brought on by Julie's behavior. I'm not sure that's fair, though. He'd pushed himself hard all his life and reached the age where it might have happened, no matter what . . .

"Anyway, he recovered from it pretty well but when Julie got married again a year later to a beatnik type—remember how we used to call them that?— who expected to live off her allowance, her father had had it. He put her share of his estate in trust until she reaches thirty-five and fixed it so that if she then wants to sell her interest in Dunham's she won't be able to force us to go public to buy her out. So you see, she has no voice in the company, plans made for expansion or whatever."

Claude finished his brandy and signaled for another. He'd had three bourbons before dinner, wine with the meal—Emily wondered if that was why he talked so freely about family affairs.

"How old is Julie now?" she asked.

"Well, this is the end of July, she'll be thirty-five in about a month, sometime around the end of August. Another Cointreau?"

"No, thank you." Emily had begun to feel a little uncomfortable over the turn the conversation had taken. Certainly some of the fault was hers that it had become so personal.

In-law personal, she reflected. Claude Whitfield had said very little about himself either tonight or the other two times they had met.

13

It was he, not his marketing manager—but didn't that just show enterprise on his part?—who had first contacted her about possible expansion into computer enclosures. He had said that his Washington distributor had told him he knew a bright girl in Falls Church, electronics distributor for several good companies, who might have some suggestions to offer on new product lines.

They'd had lunch together. He had invited her to pay a visit to Dunham's. She had driven down last week, met Paul Dunham, chairman of the board, the marketing manager and various members of the engineering staff. At lunch that day Emily had first got the impression that Claude Whitfield was attracted to her as a woman as well as interested in what Bartlett's could offer him.

She had kept the conversation on business, talking about working up a market survey questionnaire and doing some research on the demand for computer enclosures. When she left she said that she would have an estimate ready in a few days on what she would charge for the service.

Late this afternoon he had called her from Washington and suggested that they meet at a restaurant on the Virginia side of the Potomac for dinner.

She should have said she was busy tonight and would mail the estimate to him. Instead, here she was, sitting across the table from him, listening to in-law family history. The only information he had volunteered about himself was that he had first got a job at Dunham's through a friend at Hampden-Sydney College.

Emily suspected that there was no money in his

14

own family. But then, in keeping with one aspect of the American rags-to-riches tradition, he had remedied that by marrying the boss's daughter.

Had he actually fallen in love with her or was he just trying to get ahead?

While Emily speculated about this Claude Whitfield drank his second brandy and made small talk about how much pleasanter it was going out to dinner in Virginia since liquor by the drink became available.

"Used to be, we had to go to Washington for that," he added. "Now I'd just as soon stay away from there the way the niggers are out shooting and stabbing and robbing people all the time."

He saw her face stiffen and went on quickly, "Oh, sorry. Shouldn't use that word to a Yankee, should I? Should say Negroes. Although they themselves seem to prefer being called blacks these days."

"Yes, they do. Also, most of their victims are their own people," Emily pointed out, the stiffness her face showed echoing in her voice. "Other black people, not white people like us. And by the way, I'm from Iowa and don't really qualify as a Yankee."

"Oh, sorry again." Claude's laugh had a rueful sound. "I don't mean to keep putting my foot in it with you, of all people, Mrs. Bart—Emily. But you know how it is here in the South—we tend to call everyone north of the Mason-Dixon line a Yankee."

"Very provincial of you," she commented but smiled faintly, the stiffness leaving her face. No use getting offended. Claude Whitfield was as much a product—or was it prisoner?—of his environment as she was of her own, the small town in Iowa where there were no Negroes at all in her childhood and no need for the race issue to come up.

"Iowa," Claude mused aloud. "I've been talking so much about my own affairs—I said you were too good a listener, didn't I?—that I haven't given you a chance to say a word about yourself. How did you get from Iowa to Falls Church, Emily?"

He looked interested but didn't ask the name of her home town or what part of the state it was in, she noticed. Not that she intended to go into detail about her background, anyway. A business association like theirs wasn't supposed to get personal. He was a married man. . . .

"My husband picked it," she said. "We worked together getting a start. He was president of Bartlett's, I was executive vice-president." She laughed. "Sounds impressive, doesn't it, considering a staff of five people?"

She had a low soft laugh, Claude thought. A low soft voice, too, the kind of voice a real lady should have.

"How long ago was this start made?" he asked wanting to pin down her exact age.

"Oh, eight years ago for me, twelve for my husband."

That made her about ten years out of college. Thirty-one, thirty-two. Just right for him.

"And your husband died—?"

"Three years ago." Her tone closed the subject. Apparently it was still too painful for her to talk about it.

He shifted ground. "Do you have any children, Emily?"

16

"No," She spoke with the same abruptness. Another sore spot, it seemed. They had probably put off starting a family and then suddenly it was too late. Or was she, like Alix, unable to have children?

Emily reached for her pocketbook, took out a long envelope and handed it to him. "Here's the estimate I've made out if you decide to have Bartlett's do the survey for you."

There were two pages. His eye went to the bottom of the second page. The charge would be thirty-five hundred. Not too high, not a figure he couldn't talk Paul and the marketing manager into accepting.

"Let me know what you decide," Emily said, crisply matter-of-fact now. She looked at her watch. "It's past eight o'clock. I really must be on my way."

He paid the check. They went outside together and said good night in the parking lot. Emily smiled and held out her hand as he opened her car door for her. "Thank you for dinner, Mr. Whitfield," she said. "I enjoyed it very much."

"There you go forgetting again," he reproached her.

"Oh. Well then—thank you, Claude."

"My pleasure. You'll hear from me soon."

He stood back and gave her a quick little wave as she drove out of the parking lot.

Emily thought about him more than she wanted to on the way home; about his wife, too, and what kind of a marriage they had. Was it as close, as congenial as hers and Gordon's had been?

All at once she felt a sharp stab of pain, a desperate loneliness for her husband. Although she hoped she would love again and eventually remarry, she knew that in some ultimate sense she would never quite get over losing him.

But he was gone. And now there was only her empty house to go home to.

Claude waited until she was out of sight before getting into his car. He had made a mistake, he thought, asking any questions about Emily Bartlett's private life. It was too soon for that. She had that certain reserve about her. She had cut the evening short right after he had brought up her husband's death.

Or could she have had a late date? She had twice mentioned getting home.

Starting his car, he wondered how much dating she did. And why, attractive as she was, she hadn't already remarried with her husband three years dead. Still carrying a torch for him or just hadn't met the right man to take his place?

Well, he himself couldn't offer matrimony but he wouldn't mind being the right man in all other respects.

2

She was driving, of all things, a new bright-red Cadillac convertible—so ostentatious of her, Alix thought, and what had become of the Lincoln she'd been so fond of these last few years?—top down to the July sun, sweeping up over the brow of the hill and stopping short at the brick walk, power brakes squealing, gravel spraying out from under the wheels.

Alix Whitfield moved slowly, reluctantly—why should she be eager to greet a sister whose arrival invariably brought trouble, large or small?—down the front steps taking in details of Julie Dunham Lewis Norton Graham's appearance as she got out of the car; long dark hair loose and windblown, sleeveless dress halfway up her bare tanned thighs and, even worse, the deep V-neck making it all too plain that she wore no bra.

What was she thinking of, dressed like that, hair worn like that at her age?

Julie stood looking at the big brick house, Wayland, classically simple in line, built near the end of the eighteenth century by one of her maternal ancestors. The walk made of bricks as old as the house led to the front steps, shaded on either side by oak trees so massive that they might have been there before the house was built.

"Hi, Alix," she said with nothing in her tone to indicate that it was almost two years since they had seen each other. "I can't think why you insist on keeping this walk. It would be so much simpler to have the driveway circle around to the front door instead of people having to get out of their cars forty feet or more away from it regardless of the weather or any luggage they have to bring in."

"Milton will take care of yours. He's working out back somewhere and if you'll give Lily your keys she'll see that he tends to it."

"But just the same—"

"Julie, please don't start an argument before you're inside the front door. You know perfectly well that Daddy wouldn't hear of it when Claude suggested taking out the walk years ago. Neither will I."

"I know, I know." Julie brushed cheeks with her in what passed for a kiss and continued, "God forbid anything around here should be changed from Great-great-great-granddad Way's—or is it four greats?—time. It's a wonder we have indoor plumbing and electricity."

Alix caught the smell of alcohol from her sister and drew back to look at her closely. But Julie's dark eyes were as clear as her own gray ones. There were shadows under them, a trace of pallor under her summer tan, a faint air of haggardness—but still, watching her walk toward the house, Alix admitted to herself that for all Julie's undisciplined life, she didn't look within years of being in her middle thirties.

There was some spark in her not yet quenched, a pertness of expression, a gamin touch that held off age. She wasn't pretty—her looks had never compared with Alix's own pale gold beauty—but she'd always had a store of liveliness, a restless challenging vitality that had made men seek her out, as they never had Alix, since her early teens.

Well, all that would end, was bound to end, soon, Alix consoled herself as they went into the house. That first faint haggardness told the whole story. Julie's youthfulness, spent before its time, would go suddenly one of these days like a light blown out in the wind, leaving nothing but the husk of herself behind.

Alix, on the other hand, guarded her looks. Fresh air and exercise, regular hours, meticulous care of hair and complexion, moderation in all things, made up her regimen. Julie wasn't the only one to look young for her age. No one meeting Alix for the first time would ever dream that she had turned forty last month. No one. Friends who knew her age often told her that.

It still wasn't fair, though, Alix thought with a resentful glance at her sister, that Julie, careless of all the rules for healthful living, should still be holding back the years more lightly than Alix herself.

It wasn't fair. But then, nothing ever had been fair between them.

Lily, the maid, was waiting for them in the front hall. She had only been at Wayland for three years, her acquaintance with Julie therefore limited to the brief stormy visit Julie had paid them nearly two years ago, arriving drunk in the middle of the night without luggage or plans, having left Dan Graham for the second time. In that crisis he had called her the next day and a reconciliation had followed. In their present situation it seemed that he had left her. . . .

Lily, coffee-colored face impassive, greeted Julie politely. "It's nice to see you again, Miz Graham."

"Thank you, Lily. I suppose I should say it's nice to be back. Will you ask Milton to bring in my suitcases and to put the car away, too, please? The keys are in the ignition."

Suitcases plural, Alix noted as Lily said, "Yes, ma'am," and vanished down the hall. This was not to be a short stay then. She couldn't even ask if there was any time limit to it. Half the house belonged to Julie.

"My room ready?" Julie inquired.

"Yes, of course."

Julie headed for the stairs, stopped and looked down the hall. "Edna in the kitchen?"

"Starting dinner, I should think. She put a ham to soak yesterday as soon as she heard you were coming."

"I'd better say hello to her." Julie went on to the kitchen.

Edna had been the Dunham cook and Julie's confidante all her childhood days but there was no eagerness in her step as she reached the two-way door and pushed it open. Childhood was long gone; too many unhappy episodes, too many drinks, too many husbands had built a wall between old days and new. There was more sadness than joy now on Edna's chocolate brown face whenever Julie arrived for a

22

visit. Julie had been her favorite, a bright little girl brimming with mischief, teasing, loving, telling secrets to Edna.

But what was there left to say now?

They kept up pretenses with hugs and kisses and all the right words.

"Well, I declare, Miss Julie, you are a sight for sore eyes."

"And so are you, Edna. It's just wonderful to see you. How've you been keeping yourself?"

"Fine, couldn't be better."

"I don't know about that. You've gained more weight. You're eating too much of your own good cooking."

"But look at you, Miss Julie, you're not eating enough; skinny as a rail, you are. Got to fatten you up while you're here."

"Your ham and biscuits would fatten up a skeleton, Edna. My, it smells good out here."

So it went until, after a decent interval, Julie escaped, taking with her awareness of the worried note under the warmth in Edna's voice. She went up to her room, her old room overlooking the yard in back, separated from the open field beyond by Wayland's famous spirea hedge.

Her luggage, the beautiful matched pieces Dan had given her three Christmases ago, had been brought up. She said, "Oh God," under her breath as they caught her eye, then walked over to the rear window and stood looking out at the distant irregular line of High Ridge Mountains, blue with haze in the late afternoon heat.

She saw her car come around the side of the house

with Milton, Edna's husband, at the wheel. It vanished into the garage attached to the stable—no horses in it now that Daddy was dead. Nostalgic memories of herself and Daddy riding across the field touched her for a moment. Then Milton appeared, skirting around his own car, a ten-year-old Ford, spic and span with the care he gave it, and cutting across the lawn toward the house, swinging her keys in his hand.

He walked slowly—he was past sixty, must be, and Edna too—moving out of her range of vision as he approached the back door.

Julie stood back so that he wouldn't see her. She wasn't in the mood for exchanging greetings through the window; they could wait.

A little later someone knocked on her door. "Come in," she said turning to face it.

Lily entered the room and put Julie's keys down on a chest near the door.

"Miz Whitfield says maybe I could help you unpack ma'am, before I leave," she said.

She wore the same polite, closed expression Julie had noticed downstairs. No Miss Alix, Miss Julie from her. There never would be. Lily belonged to a younger generation than Edna and Milton and no easy familiarity, with its implied condescension, would sit well with her. She did the work she was paid for—did it well, probably, or Alix, who took pride in a smooth-running household, wouldn't have kept her—from ten to four, Monday through Friday, and then was picked up by her husband and went home. It was strictly an employer-employee relationship. She kept her place and expected them to keep theirs.

"No, thank you, Lily," Julie replied. "I'll unpack later myself."

The maid withdrew. As she closed the door after her Julie went over to her luggage, two suitcases and a fitted cosmetic case placed on an old pine bench that served as a luggage rack. She opened the smaller suitcase and took out a bottle of gin with only a drink or two gone from it. It would be her private supply until she got to an ABC store.

She hadn't come to drinking it straight. A cough syrup bottle with the label still on it held vermouth.

There would be glasses in the hall bathroom that no one else would use. Claude and Alix had their own bathroom off the front bedroom that had once been Daddy's and Mama's.

Not that she could really remember Mama in it. She had died when Julie was six. She was only a name, a shadow, fugitive recollections of a figure on a chaise longue — "Mama doesn't feel well today; go outside and play now, Julie, that's a good girl."

That was Mama. Daddy was entirely different, of course. Marvelous darling Daddy, her whole life once. Daddy. . . .

Julie unpacked toilet articles and took a shower. Back in her room she poured a generous measure of gin into a glass, added a splash of vermouth and locked up the two bottles in the top bureau drawer. She had a hiding place for the key, a small nail driven into the back of the mirror frame, that she had used since her girlhood days.

She drank her drink a small sip at a time to make it last while she unpacked and put on clean clothes. She was going to watch her drinking, let them see, Uncle

25

Paul, Alix and Spence Hollis, her three trustees, that in spite of her breakup with Dan (Please, God, don't let it be permanent) that she was a responsible person, perfectly able to take care of her own money when her thirty-fifth birthday came around next month.

Maybe she shouldn't have arrived so soon, nearly four weeks to go, she thought, brushing her hair and putting on lipstick. Maybe it was going to be too much of a strain. But she had to offset the news of her breakup with Dan—and then, and then, hadn't she always come back here when things went wrong? This was her heart's home. She couldn't stay in it long nowadays with holier-than-thou Alix and her kept husband but still, it was her refuge, her burrow, even without Daddy.

Daddy, who had made that horrid will—no, she mustn't look at it that way. She had been doing some crazy things at the time and Daddy, who always knew best, had tried to protect her.

Julie drained her glass. Just one more, she thought, just a swallow to steady her nerves before she went downstairs.

She heard a car arrive while she was rinsing out the glass in the bathroom and looked out the window in time to see her brother-in-law's Chrysler disappear into the garage. She made a face and returned to her room, popping a mint into her mouth to cover up, she hoped, the smell of gin.

A last look in the full-length mirror on the closet door came next. Maybe she shouldn't let her hair hang loose down her back. It wasn't, after all, quite dignified for a woman of thirty-five, seeking control of her inheritance. She gathered it together with an elastic band and pinned it up in a twist in back. Then she frowned at her image in the mirror. Long hair was a nuisance. Dan had talked her into letting it grow but tomorrow she would get it cut. A short, short haircut too.

Carpet deadened her step on the stairs. She halted on the way down hearing her name spoken in the front parlor. Claude was the speaker.

"On account of Julie?" he said sharply. "Are you suggesting that no drinks should be served the whole time she's here? Ridiculous, Alix. It wouldn't stop her in the least. Nothing stops an alcoholic. Never has, never will."

Anger flared in Julie. How dared he call her an alcoholic? She'd tell him a thing or two—

But anger died in her as quickly as it had come. By the time she reached the foot of the stairs she was ready to stop and think. Getting into a fight with Claude was no way to start her visit.

She stood and listened but couldn't quite hear what Alix said or his reply. They had moved to the far end of the front parlor or perhaps on into the back parlor. Alix sometimes called the front parlor the living room and the back parlor, with its wall of bookshelves, the library but to Julie they would always be the front and back parlors. Daddy had never called them anything else. He had laughed at Alix years ago when she said it was too old-fashioned.

After a moment Julie went into the front parlor. Claude and Alix had moved into the back parlor, Alix just inside the open double doors between the two rooms, Claude leaning against the fireplace mantel under an oil painting of Alix done five years ago.

"Hello, Claude," Julie said crisply, advancing toward them.

"Well, Julie." He wheeled around and strode over to her, warmly shaking hands and giving her a brotherly kiss. "How are you? Good to have you back."

"Good to be back." She smiled and thought what liars they were, both knowing they couldn't care less about each other.

"Lily said you didn't need her help unpacking," Alix remarked. Her tone was casual but was she guessing at the bottle in Julie's luggage?

"In Connecticut there isn't that kind of help available," Julie answered on the same casual note. "We make do with a cleaning woman twice a week, so you see I've got used to packing and unpacking for myself."

"Well, well," Claude said affably, "you've become quite the self-sufficient Yankee, Julie. By the way, I noticed you have a new car. Where's that Lincoln you thought so much of?"

Julie shrugged. "It was getting old. Seemed time for a change and they don't make convertibles any more."

No need to tell them she had hit a tree one night and totaled out the Lincoln. They'd know she was drunk at the time.

"Quite showy, your new car, the color and all," Alix said.

"Yes, isn't it? People will surely know I'm coming."

"Shall we have a drink?" Claude interposed catching glances like crossed swords passing between them.

"Fine," said Julie, and then suddenly feeling boxed in with both of them looking at her, studying her, added, "Let's have it out on the porch."

"What'll you have? Alix and I usually settle for bourbon and water."

"Martini for me," Julie replied. "Light on the vermouth."

She went out onto the porch with Alix while Claude headed for the kitchen. As she sat down she saw Milton carrying garden tools into the stable and called to him. He waved and called back and when he had put the tools away came across the lawn to speak to her.

Julie opened the screen door and went outside to shake hands with him just as Claude appeared with a tray that held the makings of their drinks. It was the worst possible moment for Milton to break off some pleasantry and say, "Oh, Miss Julie, you want that gun you brought left in your car trunk? Edna, she said not to touch it and I couldn't figure out did you want it in the house or not."

"I'll take care of it later, Milton," Julie said.

The doubtful look on his dark face did not change. He shook his head. "You watch out, Miss Julie. Mighty tricky things to have around, guns is."

He went on to the back door. Alix waited until he had gone inside and then exclaimed, "What are you doing with a gun, Julie?"

She turned from the screen door to face them, Alix sitting forward in her chair, Claude at a table fixing their drinks.

"Woman traveling alone these days might need

one," she said airily.

"What good would it do you in the trunk if someone stopped your car?"

"I usually put it in the glove compartment. Forgot it was in the trunk."

"Got a permit to travel with it?" Claude inquired, putting more vermouth than suited her into the small glass pitcher he was mixing her martini in. "Don't know about all the states you drove through but New York's got the Sullivan Law. You'd have been in real trouble if anything happened and the police caught you with it. Where'd you get hold of it anyway?"

"Doesn't matter," said Julie.

"What caliber?"

"A .32."

"And it's loaded?"

"Yes, what good otherwise?" She would not tell them, anyone, that in a black mood last night she had almost turned it on herself and finally, in horror, run outside to put it out of immediate reach in her car.

"Well, you can't leave it there in the trunk," Alix said. "That's looking for trouble."

"I'll get it out after dinner and lock it up in my bureau drawer," Julie said. "Meanwhile, let's forget it. How's Brooke?" She took the drink Claude offered her and in her nervousness gulped down half of it in one swallow.

Alix gave her a disapproving look and replied, "Brooke's fine. I ran into her downtown yesterday and told her you were coming. She said for you to call her right away."

Brooke Hollis Parker was Julie's oldest, closest friend. The same age almost to the day, they had played and gone to school together all their childhood, taken piano and dancing lessons from the same teachers. Brooks had lived just down the road then at Hollis Hill, the family home, sold now to new people.

They had roomed together at Crestwood, a girls' school in the Shenandoah Valley, sharing their whole lives until they were seventeen and Bob—Robert Hopewell Brent—sophomore at the University of Virginia came into Julie's and changed it forever.

Brooke hadn't liked him, the big smooth-talking football star, from first meeting. A phony, she had called him and they had fought over that and then—well, then it turned out that Brooke was right.

One marriage for Brooke. Only one to good solid Roger Parker, Rockwell born and bred, his father and hers law partners in the good solid firm of Hollis and Parker with Roger and Spence, Brooke's brother, now carrying on in the same remodeled old house downtown that their fathers had shared before them. Life had gone straight and true for Brooke. Two children, a devoted husband in Roger, an established niche in an established world.

Julie lit a cigarette and poured herself a refill. Claude and Alix, still on their first drink, said nothing, just looked. Let them look, thought Julie.

"I'll call Brooke now," she said.

"It's dinner hour for the children and Roger getting home," Alix pointed out. "Not a good time."

"It's always a good time for Brooke and me," Julie retorted and went into the house brushing away sudden tears that came to her eyes.

She had to look up Brooke's number. Funny, how you forgot things like that.

31

But the sense of strangeness vanished when Brooke answered, a glad note in her voice when she heard Julie's.

Brooke was the only person in Rockwell she really loved. It was sad but it was true.

Tonight, after dinner, they would see each other. Tomorrow she would visit Daddy's grave.

That was all there was left in Rockwell for her. Well, not quite. There was also Spence, dear bachelor Spence who had once been her beau. She would see him too. She was very fond of Spence, the third trustee of her money.

3

Wholesome looking, people had said of Brooke since her childhood; a pleasant kind of face. She had never minded; hadn't made any particular effort to improve on what she had in the way of looks, blue eyes, brown hair, ordinary features. You could do lots more with yourself, Julie used to protest when they reached dating age; your hairdo, make-up, lots more. But Brooke had only smiled and shrugged it off. There'd always been Roger in her life and he was satisfied with her the way she was.

Arriving at Wayland that evening with her husband and Spence, Brooke, at thirty-five, was beginning to show her age. There were fine lines around her eyes and mouth, threads of gray in her hair. The sturdiness of earlier years had turned into the comfortable plumpness of a serene matron, wife, and mother.

But there was more to Brooke than this unremarkable role suggested. She was the antithesis of Julie, not governed by impulse, inclined to think things over before she acted, but firm in carrying out a decision once she had reached it. Another major difference between them was that unlike Julie, who had never learned to laugh at herself, Brooke had a wry humor that had always kept her from taking herself too seriously.

Julie rushed out to greet her. They embraced on the

front steps and then stood back to look at each other.

"Brooke, you've put on more weight," Julie said accusingly. "You've got to go on a diet. No, maybe not. It's becoming. You look contented—if that's the way to put it."

"Contented cow," Brooke agreed cheerfully. "But Julie, honey, you're so thin yourself it's too bad I can't give you some of my excess."

"Women," said her brother Spence to Roger Parker as they waited in the background. "Can you imagine men picking each other apart like that the minute they met?"

"I should hope not," said Roger. "How are you, Julie?" He came forward to shake hands and drop a quick kiss on her cheek. Then it was Spence Hollis's turn. Stooping from his lanky height—he was as thin as his sister was plump—his kiss and handshake were more personal. Once he had been in love with Julie and built youthful dreams around her that sometimes came back to hover over him when he saw her, dim ghosts from the past.

They sat on the porch in the twilight, talking, reminiscing with the ease of old acquaintance, all except Claude Whitfield, the relative newcomer, who couldn't share their memories and so was left out of it on these occasions, giving most of his attention to tending bar.

Julie played her part, asking questions about people she had lost all interest in, if she'd ever had any, counting her drinks, bourbon now instead of gin, trying not to think of the pain she felt over her husband who had left her.

No mention was made of him by the others. They

34

were all being tactful about her unexpected visit.

But later, when Brooke got her alone upstairs in her room on the pretext of looking at a dress she had bought recently, her first question, "Julie, honey, what's wrong?" produced floods of tears and broken explanations.

Brooke listened to them with sinking heart. Julie's drinking, Dan's threats to leave her if she didn't stop, the scenes they had, the worry and embarrassment she caused him, her car totaled out three months ago with her walking away uninjured before the police could catch up with her for drunken driving, her father-in-law's disapproval of her, all of it building up into Dan's carrying out his threat to leave her three nights ago when he came home and found her passed out on their bedroom floor.

"I wanted to stop drinking," Julie said at the end. "I kept trying, I really did, Brooke, and I'd go along fine for a while but then something would set me off—"

"You'll just have to give Dan time to get over the way he feels now," counseled Brooke who liked Julie's husband, by far the best of the lot, she thought.

Julie shook her head desolately, wiping away tears. "He means it this time, I know he does. There's something immovable about him once he makes up his mind."

"Wait and see if he really has," Brooke said.

Julie got up from the bed where she had flung herself, walked across the room, turned back and said, "I'm sure he has. Which makes me a three-time loser, Brooke—or is it four, counting Bob? Sometimes when I look back on my life, I feel it was with

Bob that it all began to go wrong."

No, much earlier than that, Brooke thought. Much, much earlier when Julie was her daddy's darling, petted, spoiled, her every whim indulged, her faults glossed over or ignored while Alix had to stay in the background, keeping her feelings to herself.

"If only they'd let me have my baby," Julie continued in a fresh burst of tears. "If Alix hadn't made me have the abortion, talked Daddy into it, everything would have been different. There were ways to cover it up, pretend it was the orphan of some kin of ours or something . . . But Alix—oh God, I'll never forgive her for killing my baby, robbing me of it. Never, Brooke, never!"

The baby conceived out of wedlock—and what an old-fashioned but accurate term that was—when Julie was seventeen. Her father and Alix desperately doing what they thought was best . . .

Once again Brooke kept her thoughts to herself, Julie having never looked at it like that. She hadn't blamed her father at all—he was too perfect in her eyes to be blamed for anything—she had placed all the blame on Alix. Her cry that she would never forgive her came from the bottom of her heart. She never would. Or was it herself, hiding behind Alix, that she would never forgive?

Brooke sat down on the side of the bed, drew Julie down beside her and comforted her until her fresh burst of tears ended. Then, as if Julie were one of her children, she said, "Go wash your face and tidy yourself up. We've been away too long from the others."

Julie did as she was told.

At the head of the stairs, though, she turned back to Brooke and said pensively, "It's awful to hate your own sister, isn't it? But I do. She hates me too."

Brooke said nothing. Horace Dunham had been a tough brilliant man, highly successful in business but not a wise father, leaving behind him this legacy of rivalry and hate between his daughters.

Roger came in from the porch as Brooke and Julie headed toward it. Brooke smiled at him fondly. He was neither tough nor brilliant but he was a good husband and father who played no favorites with their two children.

"Hey, girls, you've had quite a talk," he said. "We'd better get going, Brooke. I have to be in court early tomorrow."

"I'm ready," she said, and then to Julie, "I'll call you in the morning. Maybe we can go somewhere for lunch or something."

"Fine," Julie replied as the others joined them. "Good night, Roger, Spence. See you."

She felt exhausted after her outburst upstairs and turned the other way while Alix and Claude went out front with their guests. She made herself a large bourbon on the rocks and was standing at the screen door with it when her sister and brother-in-law came back to the porch. She didn't care that they saw her having another drink, resentment overriding discretion.

It was directed at Alix, not Claude. He didn't count. He was Alix's one indulgence, aberration, whatever you wanted to call it, in her otherwise carefully ordered life; her handsome kept husband, bought with Daddy's money, advanced over the years

37

from the minor job he'd held when Alix met him to marketing manager and, since Daddy's death, to president of Dunham's.

If Claude had ever made much of a contribution to the company, Julie hadn't heard of it.

But he was important to Alix. Aside from his obvious functions as permanent escort, host at the elegant parties she gave, bed partner—although it was hard to imagine that she took much interest in sex— he was the figurehead through whom she exercised control of Dunham's while keeping up the impression that she stayed in her own feminine world. She had Uncle Paul, too, of course, but he had ideas of his own and would not dance to her tune. Claude would. Claude had to.

Maybe he didn't mind. Maybe he didn't have enough character to stand up to Alix. Or played his part without protest because he loved her. For all Julie knew, Alix's pale cold beauty suited him and the cold personality that went with it matched some void in his own. She herself knew too little about their married life to reach any conclusions on it.

With her back turned she heard Claude ask her sister if she was tired or if she'd like a nightcap before they went up to bed. Solicitous, attentive husband, that was Claude.

Was he faithful too? Alix would not forgive infidelity. He belonged to her and what was hers she kept.

That was another difference between them, Julie reflected. Everything that had ever mattered to her, she had somehow let slip through her fingers . . .

She went over to the table where she had left her cigarettes, took one out of the pack and lit it.

"You smoke too much," Alix remarked.

"Yes, don't I?" Julie held out her glass to Claude who was making Alix's nightcap. "You can sweeten mine while you're at it."

He took the glass without comment. Julie moved back to the screen door, looked out at the quiet starlit night and said over her shoulder to her sister, "I smoke too much, I drink too much, I do everything to excess, don't I, Alix? Including getting married and losing husbands. Not that you care about that." A brittle note came into her voice, echoing the resentment she felt. "You haven't even asked what happened between Dan and me."

"Did you want me to meet you at the door demanding the whole story?" Alix inquired coolly. "You know I never pry." She took the glass Claude handed her and added, "Besides, I can guess most of it, I reckon. It's a road we've all been down with you before."

"Oh, go to hell," Julie exclaimed snatching her glass from Claude as he offered it to her. "Goddamn cold fish, that's what you are and that's all you ever will be."

"Come on now, Julie, that's no way to talk to your sister," Claude said uneasily. "Here you've just arrived for a visit and—"

"Visit?" Julie interrupted hotly, her glance going from one to the other. "Maybe you both need reminding that I own half of this house and half of nearly every piece of furniture in it. I can stay here the rest of my life if I want to. That's how much of a visitor I am!"

"I only meant—" he began and was cut short this

time by Alix.

"Never mind, Claude," she said. "We all know you didn't mean it the way Julie took it. But she's had a long drive today and she's tired and upset. We'd all better go to bed."

"You go," said Julie. "I'm not ready to. I'll just sit here and look at my acres—or should I say my half-acres, Alix? No, that doesn't sound right. How should I say it, half my acres, my half of the acres?"

Her voice had risen but it didn't matter. There was no one to hear her. Edna and Milton had gone home after dinner to the last of the former slave cabins, restored and modernized for them years ago by Horace Dunham. It was out of sight and sound, a quarter of a mile away, around a bend in the dirt road that branched off the driveway and came to a dead end in their dooryard.

For the rest, there were only fields and woods between Wayland and Hollis Hill, the nearest house in the opposite direction.

"Say whatever you like," Alix replied, her voice quiet but with an undercurrent of distaste for Julie's lack of self-control. She set her glass down. "I'm going to bed. Don't forget to lock up, Claude."

"No, dear. I'll be up shortly." In the light from the hall he read the message in his wife's eyes. Stay here with Julie until she quiets down.

"Good night, Julie," Alix said from the doorway. "I hope you sleep well."

"Thank you. Good night."

Alix's departure eased the sudden pressure. Julie lit another cigarette and sat down to finish her drink. "How's everything at Dunham's?" she asked Claude and then, letting misery engulf her, did not listen.

A little later she said she thought she would go to bed herself.

She seemed manageable in her lethargy. "Oh, one thing first," Claude ventured. "Hadn't you better bring in your gun, Julie? You'll probably be using your car tomorrow and it's not a good idea to have it rolling around in the trunk. Shall I go up and get your keys?"

"Well, it could wait. But if you want to, they're on the chest."

He went upstairs and brought them down to her. Julie went out to her car herself, refusing his offer to go and get the gun for her.

He thought she handled it too casually when she came back.

"Shall I unload it for you?" he asked.

"No, let it alone," she said sharply, holding it away from him. "I'll take care of it."

"Where'd you say you were going to keep it?"

"Locked up in a bureau drawer out of harm's way. So you see"—the sharpness went out of her voice—"there's nothing to worry about."

"Hope not," he said and watched her climb the stairs, the gun dangling from her hand. He shook his head and frowned but there was nothing he could do about it, he thought, except let Alix try to handle it later if she could.

4

"So there it is," Emily Bartlett said. "More of a market for the future than one existing at present. Anticipatory—unless you have a better name for it."

"No," replied Claude from his chair beside her desk with the survey pages spread out between them. "Anticipatory puts it in a nutshell."

He was close enough to catch the faint scent of her perfume and see the fine down on her arm where the sunlight touched it. Out of the sunlight it was almost invisible. That pleased him. He didn't like his women hairy.

His women. He grinned to himself at the thought that already he regarded Emily Bartlett as his.

"The market is there, though, with all the systems-oriented companies springing up in the area," Emily continued. "And according to my salesmen, what they'll want is custom but standard enclosures—you know, something that won't make their package look as if it was just dumped in a box. A little color would help, too, instead of that deadly government gray."

He nodded, gathering up the pages and putting them into the leather folder he carried. "Lot to think about. First of all, of course, I'll have Paul and Jack Gray — you met him, remember, the day you came down? — look this over."

"Yes, I remember him." Once again Emily wondered why the whole approach hadn't been made through Gray, the marketing manager. He should at least have come up today with Claude Whitfield, she thought. For that matter, no visit was necessary from either of them. She could have mailed them the survey with the letter covering her conclusions on it.

It was all a bit odd . . .

"If you decide to expand into this field the customer we turned up in Silver Spring who's interested in about twenty-five computer enclosures might be part of your tooling-up costs," she said, adding with a smile, "A sweetener for Mr. Dunham and Mr. Gray when you take this up with them."

"Yes — although the final say, as I've mentioned before, will be mine."

Emily didn't remind him that he had also mentioned not wanting to go against Paul Dunham's judgment in using the authority he had from his wife.

His wife Alix. Wouldn't she even ask how much it would cost Dunham's to get this project started? It seemed that she would take some interest even if, as he implied, she belonged to the vanishing breed of Southern belles who didn't want to bother their pretty little heads over business.

Claude zipped up the folder and made a show of consulting his watch. "Well, what d'you know, it's almost five-thirty. I had no idea it was that late."

Emily gave him a quizzical look. His surprise was overdone. He had been right there when her recepionist-secretary left at five o'clock after asking if here was anything else to take care of.

Claude's acting had a purpose, however. "Least I can do, keeping you overtime, Emily, is buy you a drink on the way home," he said with a contrite grin.

He had teeth white as snow, she thought, and then noticed that his jaw jutted slightly. But that was better than having it recede, wasn't it?

None of her business what his jaw did.

"Thank you, that's not necessary," she answered. "I'm often here later than this. Penalty of being your own boss."

"Well then, let's just say I'd like to buy you a drink. I'm in no hurry. In fact," he injected a coaxing note, "I'm on my own, more or less. Alix and Julie have gone to a big fancy cocktail party down in Northern Neck and won't be home for another couple of hours. So you'd be doing me a favor—"

Earnest expression, blue, blue eyes under that crest of silver hair. He seemed to want her company as much as she wanted his. All the more reason for sticking to her refusal, saying she had another hour's work here at her desk—

But she heard herself say instead, "All right then. Just one. There's a place near here that won't take you out of your way."

Worse was to come, though, when they were outside. Much worse. "Seems to me that it's about time I repaid some of your hospitality, Mr.—uh—Claude," she heard herself say. "Why don't you stop by at my house and let me give you a drink there?"

"Love to," he said promptly. "You just lead the way."

Crazy, she told herself, leading the way. Crazy as a loon, she was, bringing him to her home. She couldn't pretend to anyone, least of all herself, that it was only a business courtesy.

She signaled for a right turn off Route 7 and then led him through streets of apartments and houses to what presently became a country setting on a side road with woodland on either side. She made a turn off it into a court with colonial-style townhouses built around three sides and a swimming pool and playground in back screened by trees from an apartment complex farther on.

She pulled up in the slot in front of her townhouse, the last one in a row, Claude parking beside her.

"Very nice," he commented as he got out of his car and looked around. "Quite rural to be so near the highway."

"Some land squabble among heirs keeps it from building up out here," she said as they went up to the walk to her front door. As she unlocked the door she inquired hopefully, "Lawsuits over estates can run on for years, can't they?"

He laughed. "Unless the heirs have the good sense to settle out of court."

"I've been told they're too mad at each other," she said going into the hall ahead of him.

Air conditioning enveloped them in coolness as Claude followed her in and closed the door on the heat of the August day.

He took in his surroundings and because his mind ran that way, thought, She's not hurting for money. There was a large dining room on one side of the center hall with the kitchen in back, partly visible through the doorway between. On the opposite side a living room ran the length of the house with a fireplace and bookshelves along the outer wall. A powder room, toward the rear of the hall and presumably three bedrooms upstairs.

He went into the living room with Emily ahead of him. Comfortable, restful looking, lots of blues, good furniture, sliding glass door in the rear opening onto a terrace with plantings and a wood divider separating it from its next-door neighbor.

"It's like a private house, soon as you're inside," he said walking around the room and looking out the glass door. "It's just great, Emily. Do you own or rent?"

"As long as I pay my mortgage regularly it's mine," she replied. "Sit down and I'll make us a drink."

But Claude followed her out to the roomy wood-paneled kitchen with its built-in appliances and breakfast corner overlooking the terrace. "Let me help you," he said.

She got out liquor, glasses, and ice, and then put crackers and cheese on a plate while he made the drinks.

"Shall we sit outside?" she suggested.

"And waste your air conditioning?"

"It's cool out there, too, this time of day, with the sun gone from it," she said, preferring the openness of the terrace to a living room tête-à-tête with him.

But Claude shook his head. They were at cross purposes. The greater intimacy of the living room was just what he wanted.

He sensed her uneasiness, though, over having him there and made it a point to talk business for the first few minutes after they were settled with their drinks.

The shift away from it was gradual but by the time they were ready for a second drink Emily felt free to ask if Julie planned to go back to Connecticut soon.

"No prospect of it," he replied. "She calls her husband about once a week but it seems he doesn't want her back and tells her so."

"Poor Julie," said Emily.

"Yes, but if she loves him so much, it's too bad she's made his life a perfect hell with her drinking. Reckon there's nothing she hasn't done to drive him away — except, maybe, shoot him with that gun she got hold of somewhere."

"Gun?"

"Yes indeed. Locked up in her bureau drawer. She won't even take the bullets out of it."

"That seems rather dangerous with an unstable person like her."

"Not as bad as it sounds. Julie carries on a lot but I doubt she's about to shoot either Alix or me."

"I was thinking more of her getting in the mood to shoot herself."

Claude shrugged. "Not likely. She takes her feelings out making scenes."

"Even so, it doesn't seem right that she has access to a loaded gun," Emily persisted. "Can't your wife do something about it?"

"Not a chance. She's the last person Julie would listen to." Claude hesitated and then went on: "They're nothing alike, you see. You'd never guess they were sisters in looks or personalities or any way at all. When Julie carries on, Alix just gets colder. She may say some needling thing but she won't be drawn into the kind of down-to-earth fight most sisters seem to have. I don't know—" Claude broke off, took a swallow of his drink and added in a burst of frustration, "God, you can't imagine what it's like being caught in the middle between the two of them! I'd like to see Alix end Julie's trust on her birthday this month and give her control of her money just to get rid of her. But Alix says it would be a negation of their father's intent to protect Julie from herself; that she'd throw away the money with both hands and land back on us within a year."

"I guess that could happen," Emily said, although she didn't want to agree with Alix over anything. A picture of her was emerging; cold, selfish, lacking sympathy for poor mixed-up Julie, her major concern in retaining control of her sister's money the fear that she might become a burden after spending it or, even worse, a liking maybe for the sense of power her control of it gave her.

But before this picture of Alix could take shape the thought came to Emily that it didn't fit in with her earlier concept of Claude's wife as an emptyheaded Southern belle who took no interest in the family business.

Perhaps it did, though. Alix didn't have to be interested in the source of the money to want to control all she could of it.

Still, it was somehow, confusing . . .

Claude finished his drink and stood up, saying penitently, "I should be ashamed of myself, Emily, the way I keep unloading family problems on you. You shouldn't let me. You shouldn't sit there with that sympathetic expression—"

He went over to her, took both her hands in his and drew her to her feet. Emily tried to pull herself free but he held her hands tight and assumed the small-boy rueful look that even Alix, who knew so well the shortcomings the look could cover, hadn't always been able to resist. He spoke impetuously, words pouring out as if unrehearsed.

"You don't know how much it means to me being here like this," he said. "Your friendship, the sense of peace and comfort you give me. It's so different from what home is like these days—the constant friction, the scenes Julie makes with Alix needling her on—me in the middle somewhere—Christ knows where—"

Emily tensed but no longer tried to pull herself free. Her eyes, her expressive brown eyes that turned out to be hazel flecked with gold at close range, betrayed something of the conflict inside her between the sympathy she felt for him and awareness that she had no right to feel it or listen to him at all, a married man who should remain no more than a business acquaintance.

He let her go, turned toward the door and said humbly, "I'm sorry, Emily. Thank you for having me here. I didn't mean to—"

She kept her distance walking out into the hall with him, all too conscious of his maleness, the sudden intense physical magnetism that had sprung up between them while he held her hands. Then, at the door, she regained her composure, gave him an uncertain smile and said, "Cheer up, Claude. You weren't that bad. And we all have to let ourselves go sometimes, don't we?"

"Emily girl." His rueful look vanished. "You are an

angel, you know." He let his glance be drawn to her mouth, a generous, giving mouth, lips slightly parted.

But he resisted the temptation to kiss her. The uncertainty she revealed warned him not to rush her. She was worth waiting for; he couldn't remember when he had wanted a woman so much.

He wouldn't even mention seeing her again. He would have to work it out first, anyway, an evening when he could get away from Alix.

So he said good-by and instead of shaking hands when Emily offered hers raised it to his lips.

The next moment he was gone, silvery hair glinting in the sun as he went down the walk.

Emily closed the door and moved slowly back into the living room, quiet now and somehow forlorn. She looked at the hand Claude had kissed and raised it to her lips seeking the exact spot his own had touched.

Then she said aloud impatiently, "Stop acting like a silly kid. He's married. He's a dead end street. Keep away from him from now on."

Her voice choked up with tears. She dropped down on the sofa, not knowing whether she cried over herself, the lonely quiet of her house, over Gordon who was dead and gone forever, or over Claude Whitfield who was married and had been for years.

5

"Last night was the limit," Alix said. "Passing out cold at the Clarksons' party. Claude and Spence both tried to get you out of there before you disgraced yourself completely but nobody could do anything with you. You behaved dreadfully, your language and all, in front of everyone, including those people from Richmond we'd never met before. I thought I'd die of embarrassment."

"Sorry," muttered Julie.

"Sorry's not good enough. It's got to stop, Julie. You have no right to come down here and shame us like that in front of our friends."

They were at lunch, although for Julie, barefoot and unkempt in an old cotton robe, it was breakfast. Alix, however, going out to play bridge that afternoon, was perfectly groomed, hair freshly done, crisp blue linen dress setting off her golden tan, her snowy white gloves and pocketbook on a chair by the door.

Julie nursed her hangover, pouring iced tea into herself but only toying with the fruit salad Edna had set in front of her. Alix's cool precise enumeration of her sins did not help.

If she would just once be kind, Julie thought, with a sudden lump in her throat. If she would just once say she knew how unhappy Julie was and that she wished there was something she could do about it. Just once.

But she never would. She went on talking about how unforgivable last night's behavior was. She could just imagine, she said, how all her friends were talking about it today. She didn't know how she was going to face the ones who would be at the bridge party this afternoon.

"Some of them were my friends too," Julie said at last, rousing to defend herself. "Maybe they'll be more charitable toward me than you, my own sister."

"Brooke, you mean?" Alix inquired on the same cool note. "She's about the only friend you have left in Rockwell. You've driven all the rest away."

Julie didn't answer. She laid down her fork, her queasy stomach rebelling at food, wanted nothing but liquid put into it. Milk would be soothing.

She rang the handbell. Lily appeared and was asked to bring her a tall glass of milk.

But it was Edna who brought it, face like a thundercloud. She knew about last night, of course. She had been long home and in bed before Spence carried Julie into the house but she knew just the same, probably before she came to work this morning. Her people had their own grapevine. They knew things before the white people they worked for did. Julie had disgraced Edna too.

She drank her milk slowly, letting its coldness refresh her parched throat.

Alix got up from the table eyeing her with distaste.

54

"Will you please finish that and go back upstairs before Ruth Franklin comes by for me? You look a perfect sight."

"Do I? That makes us a pair. Me a perfect sight, you a perfect bitch. There's only one way to break up the act, Alix. Give me my money next week and I'll go away, leaving you and your kept husband in full possession of the house, my half, your half."

"That's a decision I can't make by myself," Alix retorted tight-lipped with anger. "I'm only one of the trustees."

Julie stood up, hands propped on the table as she leaned across it glaring at her sister. "So that's the way you're going to play it—not your decision, eh? Well, we both know better. We both know that Uncle Paul will follow your lead and that Spence will be ready to leave the final decision to you in a family matter like this."

"Will he? Aren't you forgetting that he saw the condition you were in last night? Don't you think that will carry more weight with him than anything I might say?"

Alix paused to let the barb sink in and then concluded tartly, "He's seen you drinking ever since you came. He knows what you are—an irresponsible alcoholic lacking the decency to even try to cover it up."

Edna, alone in the kitchen with Lily back upstairs, listened at the dining-room door, shook her head sadly and moved away. "It's purely sinful, them two hating each other so," she mumbled to herself as she stacked dishes in the dishwasher. "Their daddy's doing, I always said. Yes, Mistuh Horace"—Horace

55

Dunham might have been standing beside the sink from the way Edna turned as if to speak directly to him—"you made big mistakes raising them motherless girls. What's to come of it now, I ask you? What's to come of it?"

Alix and Julie went out into the hall as a car drove up outside, Julie halting at the foot of the stairs, Alix going to the door and calling through the screen, "I'll be right out, Ruth."

Julie watched her sister put on her gloves, smoothing down each finger of them meticulously, and said, "I have one more thing to tell you, Alix, if you'll just forget your damn gloves for a minute—you'll be the last woman in America to give up wearing them, won't you?—and listen to me. I want you to understand that I'm staying here in this house until you turn my money over to me, every cent of it. Meanwhile, you can just start figuring out my share of the expenses, one-third of everything it costs to run this place. And when it's fall"—she started up the stairs, stopped and looked back—"add on my share of the heating bill too. Because I'll still be here, right here, where I've got every right to be. And there's nothing you can do about it except give me my money."

She moved up another step and added over her shoulder, "Don't start talking about what's in my best interests either. You know perfectly well that if I spent everything that's coming to me outright, I still wouldn't end up in the poorhouse. I'd have income from my share of Dunham's and I'd have my husband. He can refuse to live with me but he can't let me starve. So just think about that when you're making your decision and tell Uncle Paul and Spence

56

to think about it too."

Alix didn't answer her. She just stood there near the door while Julie ran up the last few steps. A frown marred the perfect oval of her face. She put up a gloved hand to smooth it away. But the bitter taste of anger stayed in her mouth going out to the car.

Julie went straight to her room. While she was downstairs Lily had made her bed and brought order out of the chaos she had left behind her.

The phone rang as she closed the door. Let Lily answer it on one of the other extensions. Most of them, like Julie's, were portable phones. The one permanent phone downstairs in the back parlor was connected with Claude's private line in his office, a gadget that made him feel important, Julie thought.

Someone answered on the second ring. Shortly afterward, Lily knocked on her door. "Call for you, Miz Graham," she said.

Julie picked up. It was Brooke asking her to dinner but not asking her how she felt. Brooke wouldn't mention what had happened last night unless Julie mentioned it first.

Dear tactful Brooke. Much pleasanter to sit at table with Roger and her than with Claude and Alix.

"Love to," Julie said. "What time?"

"Oh, let's make it around six-thirty so I can feed the kids first and allow time for us to sit outside and have a drink."

"Fine. I'll see you then."

Julie hung up. She'd take a shower and try to take a nap. Maybe she would feel better then.

She took a shower, dried and combed her hair, got into a clean nightgown and lay down on her bed. Her room was pleasantly dim and cool with the shades drawn and a small breeze flapping them now and again.

But she couldn't sleep. When she closed her eyes the phantoms of failure and despair that haunted her waking hours were still there. More and more of them every day, it seemed, only exorcised by alcohol, enough of it to bring oblivion.

But then there was the day after to face, as today . . .

She sat up on the edge of the bed and said her husband's name aloud. "Dan. Dan darling."

There was the same silence that there had been in their house in Connecticut after he had left her; the same phantoms from which she had fled back to her beginnings.

But here there were phantoms too.

Julie stood up and went over to the bureau reaching behind it for the key to the top drawer. She had switched from gin to bourbon in her private supply. She got out the bottle and a shot glass and poured a drink, stopping in front of the mirror to watch herself toss it off.

Daddy's little girl, secret drinker, public drinker.

She turned away from her image. It was too depressing, drawn face and shadowed eyes. Daddy's little girl.

The dimness of the room made it worse. She raised the shades on the three windows flooding it with sunlight.

She would allow herself one more drink, this time with water added.

Across the hall to the bathroom and back with an

inch of water in a glass. Bourbon poured in, the drink sipped to show restraint.

Dan's voice inside her head. "I'm warning you, Julie, that I've had it with your drinking. If you don't stop I'll leave you."

She didn't really believe it but it frightened her into drinking more. And then he had left her, Dan, her husband, whom she loved. They were finished, he said.

Finished. A doom-sounding word. The end of something—like their marriage, like her two previous marriages, like Bob when she was seventeen.

She sat down by a window. She could still summon up Bob's face, square-jawed, muscles showing through the ruddy skin. Bright brown eyes, lively, merry—shallow, although she hadn't known that then—thatch of red hair, big shoulders, big body of a star halfback. Bob, caught fast in her memory at the age of twenty, never seen since, untouched by time.

The first man she went to bed with, feeling as if she owned the world, above all, Bob himself.

She could remember everything about his appearance but nothing about his lovemaking except that it didn't measure up to what she had expected of it.

But he drove over to school to see her weekends and took her out, everyone thought he was wonderful, that she had caught a prize, everyone except Brooke.

Christmas vacation spelled uneasiness, waiting, telling herself it would be all right. Then there was Bob coming to stay over New Year's and it still wasn't all right. Telling him on the way home from the dance at the club that she was three weeks overdue on her period. Bob saying, We'll drive to Washington tomorrow, you can have that rabbit test. Nothing to worry about, I've been too careful every time we've been together, nothing to worry about but you have that test just to make you feel better.

Something wary in his tone, though, some drawing back, separating himself from the knot of worry she carried around, making it all hers, nothing to do with him.

The test positive. The drive back, Bob cross-examining her, saying, I've been so damn careful, I don't see how it could have happened, over and over until she flared up and asked if he thought she had been sleeping with someone else.

Quick denial of that but still looking thoughtful. Not saying then or later, It's all right, Julie, we'll go to Elkton, Maryland, tomorrow and get married. Saying instead, We'll think of something, we'll work it out.

Dinner that night slow torture, Daddy cheerfully talking football with Bob, Alix entertaining her own dinner guest, Mike Walker, a perfect creep who had hung around for years expecting to marry her until she met Claude—Alix had never had a really worthwhile beau in her life, but then, Julie hadn't had many herself who were much better until Dan came along—Edna, younger and sprier in those days, back and forth serving, candles on the table, fire crackling on the hearth, nothing different on the surface from other nights when there'd been dinner guests and yet everything different and never to be the same again.

Alone finally in the back parlor with Bob but he wouldn't talk about what she still thought of as their problem. He had a bottle in his suitcase, got ice and glasses and water from the kitchen after Edna left and made them drinks. You're tired, he'd said. We're both tired. It's been a hell of a day. Let's go to bed early and sleep on it and tomorrow we'll decide what to do.

All the time he knew what he was going to do himself. All the time.

She was dead tired that night. Daddy had let her have a glass of sherry before dinner and then she had two drinks with Bob. She wasn't much used to liquor then and could hardly keep her eyes open over her second drink. She had gone up to bed and slept like a log until eleven the next morning.

The guest-room door was open, someone moving around inside, when she went to the door to say good morning.

The bed stripped, Sally, their maid in those days, tidying up the room. Where was Bob who wasn't supposed to leave until tomorrow?

Up early and gone, Sally said. Got a phone call, he said, and had to leave. Must have got it before I came this morning, 'cause it wasn't after. Left a note for you right here, Miss Julie.

Thank you, she said, and took the note back to her room, knowing before she tore open the envelope that Bob had run out on her.

Dear Julie, the note began. *I've been thinking over what we found out yesterday and the more I thought about it, the more I was convinced that I just couldn't be the one responsible for what happened to you. I was always much too careful. You say there was no one else but there must have been. I suggest you get together with him, whoever it is, and see if you can't*

61

work something out together. I certainly hope you
can. Thanks for your hospitality and the best of luck
anyways. Bob.

Words engraved forever on her mind written by the
man she was in love with and thought she was loved
by in return. Words she had read over and over, not
quite able to believe them then and sometimes not
even now.

She hadn't cried all that day. Not until the evening
after Edna and Milton had left and she was alone
with Daddy and Alix and told them she was pregnant
and brought out the note.

Daddy like a madman at first, raving about Julie's
honor, threatening to shoot Bob with one breath and
to force him to marry her the next.

Julie crying, protesting that she would rather die than
marry Bob after the way he had treated her; that she
would kill herself if Daddy said another word about
it.

Alix quiet, watchful in the background, at last
saying the inexcusable, You are sure he's the one,
Julie? We must know the truth. Was there ever
anyone else at all?

Coldblooded, heartless Alix, superior in awareness
of her own virgin state.

Julie screamed bitch, bitch, bitch at her, hurled an
ash tray at her head. Alix ducked and let it smash
against the wall.

Daddy grabbed Julie and she collapsed in his arms.

He found a sedative pill somewhere, put her to bed
and sat with her until she fell asleep.

They must have talked half the night after that,
Daddy and Alix, Alix deciding then, but keeping to

herself, what she would insist upon.

She brought it out the next day when the three of them were shut in the back parlor to talk in privacy. Abortion was the only answer, she said. No, no, Julie said. No indeed, Daddy said, I won't hear of the risk. It will have to be adoption.

New York abortion, Alix said. A girl at college had one of them. The expensive kind. A clinic. Every safeguard.

Daddy and Julie held out for hours. They talked about a trip somewhere in the spring, Europe maybe, or somewhere out West. Then adoption, Daddy said.

No, Julie said. Please, Daddy, we can figure out some way to keep my baby, fix up some story about a cousin who left it an orphan.

No one would believe it, Alix said.

I couldn't give up my baby and never see it again, Julie said.

You see, Alix said to Daddy. Abortion is the only answer. And called her college friend and got the address in New York . . .

Right up until the time they arrived at the clinic, Daddy kept balking. In fact, right up until the moment he met the doctor in his immaculate white and saw the immaculate white room and the immaculate starched nurse who would assist. Right up until that moment it was touch and go whether Daddy would let Julie go through with it.

Julie herself had stopped fighting, balking the day before they left for New York. She was passive in acceptance, not caring any more.

At this early stage, the doctor said examining her, no real problem. Look at it, he said, as little more than a D and C, if you know what that means, Julie.

Yes, I know, she said.

The arrangements were made for the next morning, Daddy and Alix taking her back to the discreet immaculate clinic, Julie having the abortion.

Two days later they were back home and in another forty-eight hours Julie was back at school, arriving late because she was supposed to have had the flu. She would get along fine, the doctor had said, there'd be no ill effects at all.

He meant, of course, no physical ill effects. But all these years later the ill effects to her spirit, her emotional structure, whatever she should call it, were still with her and would never, it seemed, go away.

She had let them kill her baby. Alix had made her do it. Not Daddy. He would never have gone ahead with it except for Alix.

Daddy, six years now in his grave; Alix, spiteful in her grief after his funeral, saying Julie had helped put him there.

It wasn't true. It couldn't be. Alix was just being as spiteful as she always was.

Julie sprang up from her chair. No use brooding over old sorrows past changing. Have another drink, just one more very light one.

After she had it, she lay down and fell asleep until it was time to get dressed and go to Brooke's for dinner. And in her sleep she cried.

6

They met at two o'clock at Spence's office on Julie's birthday.

Julie took pains to look her best that day, fresh and alert, when she left Wayland with Alix at quarter of two to attend the meeting. She'd had nothing to drink, Alix noted, as they cut across the lawn to the garage. A different person might have had a wry smile for Julie's eleventh-hour attempt to proclaim herself competent to take control of her inheritance but Alix, like Julie herself, lacked the grace of humor.

They went in her car. Julie tried once more on the way to find out what the trustees' decision was to be but Alix, as she had all along, refused to commit herself, saying it wouldn't be proper to talk about it ahead of the meeting.

"Must be marvelous to always do the proper thing," Julie said at last with heavy irony. "Tell me what it feels like, Alix."

"Oh, stop it," said her sister and the rest of the drive was made in unfriendly silence.

But Julie still hoped against hope for a favorable decision. Not because she could even remotely rest her case on her own good behavior but on the opposite grounds of being a nuisance to have around. Alix had made it plain that she would like nothing better than to see the last of her and it was Julie's hope that she would influence the others to that end. It was what she herself would have done in Alix's place.

But she reckoned without her sister's determination to carry out her father's intent, regardless of personal inclination. Alix had spent her whole life being dutiful to him, never causing him any worry beyond concern that she insisted on marrying Claude Whitfield whom he suspected of being a fortune hunter. In return she received lukewarm affection with respect for her business acumen added in her adulthood. The light in their father's eye, the special warmth in his voice were reserved for Julie who could twist him around her little finger and who, in the end, broke his heart.

Or so Alix thought. And in spite of Julie's behavior only some ultimate sense of fairness had kept him from making a will that left more than half of his estate to his favorite daughter.

Their Uncle Paul was at Spence's office ahead of them. A spare, dry bachelor, he didn't much like Alix and thoroughly disapproved of Julie, but greeted them both with courtly politeness and when they were all seated said immediately in his precise voice, "Well, Spencer, you're the lawyer here, so why don't you render the verdict?"

Spence wasn't ready to come straight to the point. He avoided Julie's eye as he opened a file on his desk.

"I have a copy of your daddy's will here, Julie, and

perhaps I'd better refresh your memory on the discretionary trust he set up for you." He gave her a constrained smile. "Reckon you've forgotten some of it by this time. After all, he's been gone six years."

"I haven't forgotten what's important," Julie replied, two spots of color showing on her cheeks. "The way you're all acting"—her glance challenged them in turn—"it looks like you don't want to give me my money."

"Well, let's get it all clear," Spence said fiddling with the papers. "You'll recall that aside from charitable bequests and a few legacies such as Edna and Milton's, he left his entire estate to you and Alix, share and share alike. Alix's half came to her as soon as the estate was settled. But your daddy wanted you to steady down a little . . ."

Spence paused, resorting to the text in front of him to read aloud, "Whereas, in view of certain circumstances involving my daughter, Julie Dunham Lewis—" Spence paused again. "Right after your first divorce, wasn't it?"

"Yes," said Julie, color deepening with awareness that they were all reviewing the scandalous details of it in their minds.

"—I consider it to be in my said daughter, Julie Dunham Lewis's best interests that—"

"Heaven's sake, Spence," Julie interrupted impatiently, "you don't have to go through all the whereases and herebys for my benefit. I know what the will says. Daddy appointed you and Uncle Paul and Alix to take care of my money until I was thirty-five. Today is my thirty-fifth birthday and so I should get it."

"You know it's not that simple, Julie," Spence said. "You know the will gives us, the trustees, the right to decide whether it's to your advantage to extend the trust to your fortieth birthday. It's within our power to do so. At that time, your daddy felt, the corpus of the trust should go to you unless you were legally judged incompetent — in which case the court would appoint trustees of its own choice. So that's where the matter stands as of today, Julie."

"And what decision has been reached, Spence?"

"To continue the trust for another five years. Believe me, Julie" — he gave her a troubled look — "it wasn't reached lightly. We've all talked it over, given it a lot of thought —"

"I'm sure you have," Julie cut in, her voice hard with anger. "Shaking your heads over me, so sure of yourselves, so holier-than-thou — maybe I'll just get me another lawyer and take you all into court and find out if you can get away with this."

"Julie, don't even think of it." Spence got up from his desk and went over to her, his thin serious face even more troubled. "Your position isn't that sound. It's better let alone, Julie, much better. You already receive the income from your share so what's to be gained by trying to force the issue?"

He bent over her pleadingly and went on talking in that vein. Paul Dunham joined in with the reminder that her daddy wouldn't like her to go against his wishes.

"He arranged it for your protection, girl, you know that," Uncle Paul said. "You were flying pretty high, time he had the will drawn. He told me his thoughts on it, type of people you were mixed up with and all.

Like Spence says, Julie, let it alone. Don't go against your daddy's wishes."

That was the approach to take with Julie. Not the legal difficulties, Spence had brought up, but Daddy's wishes. He had wanted to do what was best for her.

"Alix had her hand in it somewhere, though," Julie said at last with a bitter glance at her sister. "Oh God, I could kill you sometimes, Alix, I really could. You and that quiet twisty way of yours that always comes out sounding so sensible—"

Alix was silent knowing that anything she might say would only fan Julie's anger. Let her make all the fuss she wanted to, just so that she didn't disgrace herself and the rest of them going to law over it. This was Alix's thought, sitting with ankles crossed, gloved hands clasped in her lap, sunlight touching her pale gold hair, her face without expression as her cool gray eyes met the bitter glance Julie gave her.

It went on a while longer, Julie gradually yielding ground, knowing in her heart that she had no chance of winning if she took it to court, shaking her head mutely at the end when Spence suggested it might make her feel better to get another lawyer's opinion on what kind of a case she had.

All her hopes, pinned on Alix's desire to get rid of her, had come to nothing.

She made a last thrust at her sister as they stood up to leave, saying to Spence, "Actually, of course, this pious concern for my welfare is just a joke, coming from Alix. What really matters to her is to go on being big boss at Dunham's by keeping me from having any voice in my half ownership of it."

"Now, Julie," Spence said uncomfortably. "That won't do."

"Indeed not," said Uncle Paul in his driest tone. "In the first place, neither one of you owns half of Dunham's. Ten per cent of the stock—non-voting, but still, ten per cent—is owned by employees under the stock purchase plan your father and I set up twelve years ago. Then, I happen to own one-fourth of the remainder. What you own, Julie, is half of what's left which is something like two-thirds of the whole."

"Oh, Uncle Paul, you know what I mean," Julie protested. "Who cares about technicalities?"

"I do," said her uncle. "Very much so."

Alix added no word in her own defense. "We'd better go, Julie," she said moving toward the door. "We've taken up enough of Spence's time already."

"I'd rather have Uncle Paul give me a ride home," Julie replied.

"Suit yourself." Alix said good-by to the others and left.

Her car was vanishing around the corner when Julie and Paul Dunham went out to his. He tried to make small talk on the way home but Julie, in a morose mood, answered in monosyllables. Going up the driveway to Wayland she roused herself to ask him in for a drink but he said no, he was returning to the plant.

"I asked Claude not to leave until I got back," he explained. "He's got this bee in his bonnet that we ought to expand into computer enclosures but I'm not much taken with some figures on it that came in from engineering today just before I left."

Julie didn't listen as he grumbled about Claude and his grandiose ideas.

She said good-by out in front and went straight up to her room. It had been an unpleasant afternoon. She needed a drink.

"That's my sister Alix over there," Julie informed the new man in town in a clear, carrying voice. "Otherwise known as Mrs. Claude Whitfield. She's a pillar of the community. She also kills babies."

It was a week after the meeting at Spence's office. As much peace as there ever was between the sisters had been restored. They were at the Labor Day dinner dance at the club, Alix and Claude with a group of their friends, Julie with Spence, Brooke and Roger with the new man in town brought along as their guest.

He had been attentive to Julie all evening. She had seemed to be in the best of spirits, more like the Julie of long ago, Brooke thought, than she had been all summer. But now this.

The new man looked startled and then nonplused. His glance went to Alix, dropping quickly when he saw that her face was frozen in anger and that everyone in her group was looking their way.

The music started again, ending the awkward moment.

"Our dance, Julie," Spence Hollis said firmly, leading her out onto the dance floor.

"For God's sake, why do you have to spoil a pleasant evening with that kind of remark?" he demanded as soon as they were clear of the others.

"Why? You haven't even had that much to drink tonight."

She shrugged, matching her step to his and said, "Maybe I can't help it, Spence. Maybe I'm just a spoiler by nature."

"Oh, cut it out, Julie." He gave her a little shake. "You going to spend the rest of your life telling everyone you meet about the abortion you had nearly eighteen years ago? That's a real dead horse you're flogging, honey, and one that's way behind the times too. It's getting so that abortions are legal all over the country. You can hardly pick up the paper without reading something about them."

Julie didn't answer. Her glance drifted to a girl across the room, radiantly pretty, no more than seventeen or eighteen, about the age her baby would be now.

If she'd been allowed to have it, she would have liked it to be a girl . . .

Or if she had shown Dan she could straighten herself out, she might have had a baby by him.

Dan, she thought in sudden desolation of spirit. Oh Dan, don't leave me forever. I can't live without you. I can't. I won't.

7

Uncle Paul was invited to Sunday dinner the day after the dance at the club. Alix planned it for four o'clock to give him and Claude plenty of leeway for whatever time they arranged their golf games that day.

Uncle Paul, however, always played early in the morning and would have liked to have had his Sunday dinner at his usual one o'clock, a routine that suited him and suited Ralph, his houseman, who then had the rest of the afternoon off.

Three hours was a long time to keep a man waiting, he thought, but didn't let his disgruntlement show, sitting on the porch with Alix, drinking his bourbon but waving aside hors d'oeuvres that might spoil the good appetite he had worked up.

"Where's Julie?" he inquired presently, mellowed by Wild Turkey and the reflection that Alix set a table as good as her liquor, he had to give her that much credit.

"Gone out to dinner somewhere with the Parkers and a man they had with them at the dance last night."

"Oh yes, the dance." Uncle Paul never attended the club's social events himself. He never had, even when he was a lot younger, but nowadays he complained that it was because they were letting so many new people join that he didn't know who half of them were, to say nothing of being able to place them through their fathers or grandfathers. For him the club was for playing golf and afterward going into the bar where everyone kept their own labeled bottles and having a drink or two with the rest of his foursome — always old friends whose fathers and grandfathers were firmly placed in his mind — and then going home to the peace and quiet of his bachelor quarters with Ralph to look after him.

"Pretty day," he said looking out over the sunlit lawn and then stealing a glance at his watch. It was quarter of four. "Claude should be along soon, shouldn't he? What time was he playing today?"

"Oh, didn't I tell you he's not playing at all? Let me sweeten your drink, Uncle Paul."

Alix took his glass and went over to the liquor table. "Claude's at the plant, putting in some last-minute work on the figures he wants to show us. He called just before you arrived, though, and said he'd be along shortly."

"He still got that special switch or whatever it is on his phone to make it ring here?"

"Yes."

"Lot of nonsense," said Uncle Paul. "Waste of money. Never felt any need for it myself."

"Well, he seems to want to have it." Alix poured a stiff shot into her uncle's glass, added ice cubes, a little water, and handed it back to him.

She didn't sit down again herself. She walked to the end of the porch and back and then asked, "Are you absolutely sure we're right in turning down this expansion plan of Claude's, Uncle Paul? Absolutely, beyond doubt or question, sure?"

"I certainly am. Even more than I was about the formica tops for executive desks that we lost money on three or four years ago. Or the plastic office furniture that the survey showed had no market. This computer enclosure thing is much bigger. The retooling alone would cost a small fortune. I'm dead against it, right now, at least. So's Gray, so's the whole engineering department. You know you're against it yourself, Alix, and you've got twice the business sense Claude has."

"He'll be wild, though," Alix predicted resignedly. "He'll have a fit."

"Let him," said Uncle Paul uncompromisingly. "We're in business to make money, not to boost his notions of what a smart fellow he is, full of smart ideas."

"Still, I don't look forward to telling him . . . Here's his car now, Uncle Paul. You've have to back me up all the way."

"Indeed I will."

They waited until dinner was over and they were back on the porch to tell Claude that there would be no expansion into computer enclosures at Dunham's.

He refused to listen to their reasons at first. He stormed at them, arguing furiously against engineering's figures that showed the retooling alone running close to a quarter of a million. He brought Emily Bartlett into it, quoting as gospel her suggestion that they could perhaps keep the retooling under two hundred thousand. He quoted her again on the growth of electronics systems in the area and then insisted that they would miss the boat if they didn't get into the market now on the ground floor.

But no matter what he said, how hard he pushed, they remained adamant in refusal. Alix, irritated by his persistence, brought up the money Dunham's had lost on his other projects.

"But can't you see how different this one is?" he exclaimed. "What about that survey Emi—Mrs. Bartlett did on computer systems springing up around Washington? You saw it yourself, Alix."

Alix gave him the dispassionate glance that often reduced him to silence. She had not missed his quick correction of himself when he started to call Emily by her first name and for the first time wondered about her as a woman, what she looked like, how old she was.

Her irritation grew as she asked, "Did Mrs. Bartlett mention high interest rates and tight money, Claude? We don't have the ready capital to tie up in this without borrowing. Or does she know that in five years we may have to buy out Julie's interest in the company? Tell Mrs. Bartlett that the next time she comes up with her clever ideas."

"It was my idea, not hers," Claude said curtly. "I went to her. She didn't seek me out."

"Mrs. Bartlett struck me as a bright young woman and must be, running that business on her own since her husband died," Uncle Paul inserted, supplying Alix with the information that Emily was young and a widow, "but she has said nothing to indicate that we

76

would make money right away on this venture, Claude. Anticipatory market is what her survey shows. Anticipatory. If we went into this thing the money we tied up would melt away faster than our established lines could make up for it considering what business conditions are right now."

"But—"

"Look, Claude"—a note of finality came into the older man's voice—"it's no use chewing this over any more. You listen to this smart wife you've got. She don't like it. I don't. Gray's been against it from the start. So's engineering. All of us except you."

"We all know why Gray's been against it," Claude retorted. "Because it's my idea, not his. Because I had the initiative to go out and look for new product lines—"

"Which it wasn't your place to do," Alix interrupted her tone even sharper with irritation over his attitude. "Gray knows his job. Let him come up with new product lines and bring them to you and Uncle Paul."

"And also to you," Claude pointed out bitterly. "Don't forget how important your approval is. You like to play the little woman but everyone at the plant and half the town besides knows that you're the boss and I'm just your lackey, constantly held back from trying anything new or different. By God, I'm sick of the role!"

Alix let her temper go. "When you qualify for a better one, I'll be happy to see that you get it," she said icy with anger. "But not through any half-baked schemes that could cost us a quarter of a million dollars. After all, it's not your money you'd be playing with. It's mine and Julie's and Uncle Paul's. You've never had any of your own so you don't even know what it means to worry about losing it."

Claude sprang from his chair, white with rage. "All I needed was to have you throw that up at me too," he shouted. "You couldn't resist it, could you Alix? You had to rub my nose in it—!"

He slammed off the porch and ran across the lawn to the garage. A moment later, motor roaring, he backed his car out and drove away.

"Well, that was quite an exhibition," Alix said at a loss.

Her uncle got to his feet. "I'd better be going along myself," he said, and then added quietly, "Too bad you brought up money, Alix. Bad enough that he knows you hold the purse strings without saying it out loud. And in front of me."

"But sometimes he gets so uppity he needs to be put in his place," Alix defended herself.

Uncle Paul just shook his head. Alix walked out to his car with him and waited until he drove away. She wasn't too worried about Claude's feelings as she went back into the house. Maybe she had said too much but give him a little time and he would simmer down.

She had the house to herself. She cleared away the dinner dishes for Edna to do in the morning and went out onto the porch again. She made herself a light drink. Twilight came while she sat there with it, thinking about how difficult Claude had been and wondering where he had gone, rushing off like that. In a tantrum, you might say. Disgraceful for a man his age.

Later her thoughts turned to Emily Bartlett, bright young widow, on friendly enough terms with Claude for him to call her by her first name. The only thing that really mattered about it was that he had been so quick in trying to cover it up.

Was Emily Bartlett pretty as well as young and bright?

8

To Claude, arriving at Emily's in the early evening, her face seemed almost beautiful with the concern it showed for him.

He had gone straight to her door from Wayland, not stopping to call and find out if she was home or if it would inconvenience her to have him come.

For once, smarting from the scene at home, there was no calculation in Claude's approach to her.

He had long ago planned what to say if Alix turned down the project that had brought Emily and him together. Not that he expected it to happen — how could it, after all the time he had spent going over it step by step with Alix? — but still, in the remote event that her verdict was negative, he had made his plans for conveying it to Emily.

More in sorrow than in anger, Claude would place all the blame on Paul Dunham.

He had even rehearsed his lines for the occasion. "Old mossback, scared to death of anything new," he would say with a rueful headshake. "Alix can't understand why I don't just override his veto — she doesn't have much understanding of business, as I may have told you — so there's been the extra problem of getting it across to her that it would be out of the question to override Paul, a man his age, who's spent his whole life at Dunham's."

"How old is he now?" Emily was supposed to ask at that point.

"Sixty-three," Claude would reply. "Getting so close to retirement" — Emily would have no way of finding out that Uncle Paul had no thought of retirement at sixty-five — "that it seems to me the decent thing to do is to wait the old boy out."

Emily would agree. Claude would lose no stature in her eyes by not going ahead with his project.

In none of this dialogue had he ever visualized himself arriving at Emily's still smarting with anger from the deep wound Alix had inflicted on his pride; or that it would lead him to revelations about his true position at Dunham's that he would not have made under any other circumstances.

Emily tried to stop his tirade, disturbed by the hatred of Alix that came out in it, but he paid no attention. At last she stood up and said, "I'm going to make us a drink, Claude. Meanwhile, will you try to calm down? I'm afraid you're going to be sorry later for the way you're talking now."

She smiled to soften her admonishment and went out to the kitchen.

She found him still pacing the living-room floor when she returned but he had used her absence to pull himself together a little. He gave her a hesitant smile as he took his drink and said, "Sorry, Emily. I know I've talked too much. In fact, I had no right to come here at all —" His hesitancy became a tool deliberately used. "I tried to stop myself—but you're the one person in the world I felt I could come to—"

Emily couldn't help being touched by what he said. The shock of his attitude toward Alix was beginning to wear off a little. She had told herself in the kitchen not to take it too seriously, that he was just letting off steam. Alix had been awful to him. She must be an awful person.

Emily went on thinking about her, sitting down again in the living room. Her first impression had been of an empty-headed social butterfly; then had come the image of a cold-hearted, selfish sister who cared nothing about Julie's problems; now there was the shrewd careful businesswoman added to these earlier impressions.

All of them came from Claude. Which was the real Alix—or did they all combine to make the whole?

Emily waited while he finished his drink, letting him calm down some more, letting silence add its own soothing effect.

At last she said, picking her words, "I don't quite understand your wife getting so involved in your plan to expand at Dunham's. I somehow thought she took no interest in it."

Claude tried to remember all he had said that gave away too much about Alix but it was already a jumble in his mind. He shouldn't have come here, he knew, until he had himself under better control. Too late to worry about that now, however. Toning down what he had said was the best he could do.

"Just now and then," he replied. "When something big comes up like the retooling we'd have to do for computer enclosures. Paul got her ear on that two or three weeks ago. I should have got my side in first but I kept putting it off." He sighed heavily and set down his glass. "So you see, I should blame myself, not Alix, knowing what she's like, that profits are her main concern. That's her only real interest in Dunham's and it's her privilege to feel that way. I had no right to talk about her to you the way I did. I'm sorry you had to listen to it, Emily. But then, we always want to put the blame on someone else, don't we?"

Emily nodded, studying him. He assumed his contrite, small-boy look that sought forgiveness for misbehavior. It was a much pleasanter one than the black hatred of Alix that his face had shown a little while ago.

But he was still not telling the whole truth, Emily thought. Alix kept a far closer eye on Dunham's than he would ever admit. She could understand, though, why he glossed over it. No man would want to admit that his wife called the tune he danced to.

Small things that had puzzled her were explained by this new concept of Alix; the reserved attitude Paul Dunham had taken the day Emily visited the plant with Claude; Claude's bypassing of the marketing manager in initiating the survey on computer enclosures. Claude must have been hoping to prove something to Alix by such independent action.

Now she had shattered that hope, very cruelly, too, the little dream he'd tried so hard to make come true.

It might not have been the most practical dream in the world but even so, how could his wife have treated him like that?

He had the bluest eyes Emily had ever seen. And

what an irrelevant thought that was!

Without meaning to, she heard herself ask, "What does your wife look like, Claude?"

He glanced at her and quickly away for fear that his face would reveal his sense of triumph over all that her question implied.

"She's fair," he said on a detached note. "Blond hair, gray eyes, fair complexion. A little taller than you, about five seven, and about your build. Much better looking than Julie. She has a classic kind of beauty, people always say. But — well, I guess it sort of needs warming up. You know — severe?"

Cold, thought Emily. Nothing gentle about her looks.

"And Julie?" This was safer ground.

"Dark hair and eyes, darker than yours, I'd say. Kind of a pixie face, you'd call it. Sometimes she'll look a knockout and the rest of the time plain as an old shoe."

"Oh. Sounds interesting." Emily rose. "Let me make you another drink."

"Can't I help?" Claude followed her out to the kitchen and took charge. He made her drink stronger than she would have herself. She was upset, he saw, really keyed up, but trying not to show it. Was it over the things he had said about Alix or because he had come to her at all?

As he handed her drink to her he said, "There's one thing more I want to add about my wife — you must be wondering, after all I've told you, if I married her for her money —"

Emily stiffened. "That's really none of my business, Claude."

He moved swiftly as she turned toward the living room, blocking her off with one arm against the doorjamb.

"I think it is," he said softly. "I want it to be. I want you to know that I didn't marry Alix for her money. I was in love with her sixteen years ago when we met. But"—he bent his head to look straight into her eyes with all the sincerity of expression that he could summon—"I'm not going to say that the Dunham money made no difference. I don't know now, looking back, how much it mattered, or if I would have fallen for Alix without it. And that's the best answer I can give you—or myself."

"Claude, please—"

He stepped aside and let her lead the way back to the living room. He was satisfied that Emily believed him which she wouldn't have done if he had insisted that he had married Alix strictly for love. He had met the issue squarely, bringing in Alix's money but limiting its importance to him.

No one, certainly, would ever hear him say that he wouldn't have looked at her without it; that she had never been his type and never would be.

Whereas Emily . . .

Claude was right in feeling that she was favorably impressed by what he had just said, but would have been less complacent over it if he had known how much her view of him had changed.

He had no great strength of character, she thought as she sat down with her drink. He wasn't weighted down with brains or ability either. He probably couldn't have made it on his own in the business world, as she and Gordon had done.

But did all that matter? Everyone couldn't be a great success in life. Claude had other qualities that drew her to him; charm, looks, friendliness, a nice personality. He had come to her to have his hurt made better. She meant a lot to him, his coming said. He needed her.

She needed to be needed.

She must stop letting herself think of him that way, though. He was married to Alix. It didn't seem that he had much love left for her but she was still his wife . . .

A little later Emily was in his arms listening to endearments pour out of him, believing him, wanting to believe him when he said he had fallen in love with her the day they met.

He was a married man but all her senses, denied love these three years past, responded to him, drowning out reason and conscience.

He carried her upstairs.

"Which room is yours?" he asked burying his face in her hair.

9

He didn't leave until after midnight.

"My God, I didn't realize it was so late," he said when he saw the time. "It'll be one o'clock before I get home."

Emily's face told him how the remark jarred on her.

"Doesn't matter," he added quickly. "Not at all."

"You could always say car trouble."

"Reckon I could." He missed the note of irony in her voice, his thought still on the time. But as she walked to the door with him, he slipped back into the role of lover, kissing her tenderly, telling her that this had been the most wonderful night of his life.

Emily let herself relax in his arms, returning his kisses, saying yes, she would be in her office all morning tomorrow if he had a chance to call her then.

But her mood changed when he was gone, car lights vanishing around the turn out of the court. She went slowly through the hall to the kitchen and tidied it up, emptying ash trays, stacking glasses and sandwich plates in the dishwasher. Not at all a romantic aftermath, she thought wryly. If she were a young girl just embarked on a love affair, household chores would be the last thing on her mind.

But she wasn't a young girl. She was a widow in her thirties.

Upstairs, a shower took away any languor left by Claude's lovemaking. She belonged to herself, Emily Murray Bartlett, again.

Not quite, though, she acknowledged to herself, examining the firm lines of her body, yielded so willingly, in the mirror on the bathroom door. She wasn't quite the self-sufficient person she had been, or at least considered herself to be, before tonight.

But actually it went back much farther than that, she thought, getting into a nightgown and creaming her face; all the way back to the first time she'd had dinner with Claude Whitfield. Ever since that night she had been increasingly aware of him, feeling her spirits lift when she heard his voice on the phone, looking forward to every visit he paid her, every hour they spent together, whether at her office, here at her house or at some restaurant.

In other words, she had been leading up to what had happened tonight all along; she had walked into the situation with her eyes wide open.

And yet she had had inner reservations about Claude almost from the start sensing some weakness in him, some lack of judgment. He had lied or at least concealed much of the truth from her about the secondary role he played at Dunham's. He had shown little loyalty or respect for his wife tonight even though anger might excuse some of the things he had said about her.

This was the man she had fallen in love with.

But we don't necessarily love people for their strengths, Emily reminded herself as she brushed her hair. It was for their weaknesses as often as not, wasn't it?

Yes, came the answer. At least with Claude. He brought out her mother instinct or some other protective instinct in her. Especially tonight when he came to her from a cold-hearted wife who had just torn his pride into shreds.

So now Emily had put herself in the position of the other woman in love with a man whom she perhaps understood all too well.

Did Alix measure him, too, and find him wanting? There had to be two sides to the story, of course. But no matter what hers was, she needn't have cut Claude down as cruelly as she had today.

Now he would have Emily to bind up the wounds she inflicted on him. Emily knew, looking at herself somberly in the mirror while she brushed her hair, that she wouldn't stop seeing Claude immediately as she should. She wanted him to come back. She wanted him to make love to her again. He was a wonderful lover.

Which meant that she didn't have much strength of character herself, she thought. She had fallen in love with a married man who hurried out into the night to get back to his lawful wedded wife, thinking up excuses for his lateness on the way.

He had mentioned divorce tonight in the midst of their lovemaking. Meeting Emily had opened up a whole new world to him, he had said; and that he felt as if he could no longer go on in a marriage of habit, convenience, whatever it should be called, with Alix.

Emily had told him not to talk like that. But she doubted that he understood how much it humiliated her or why it should.

There would be many things he wouldn't understand in their relationship. There would be happy times in it but they would be shadowed by the price she would have to pay for them through her own uncertainties and loss of self-respect.

Even now, at the very beginning of their affair, the question of how much of her response to Claude was based on loneliness and the need to be loved was already in her mind. She would try to keep it in the background but it was there.

The somber expression remained on her face as she went on looking at herself in the mirror.

"You're making the worst mistake of your life," she told herself but knew as she said it that she didn't quite believe it was true.

Alix, still awake, was reading in bed when Claude arrived home.

"Well," she said as he came into their room.

"Hi." His tone was curt. For once he had her at a disadvantage and meant to make the most of it.

He did not look at her as he began to undress.

Alix, her loosened hair haloed in the pool of light from the lamp between their twin beds, put down her book and looked at him.

"That was pretty childish of you, Claude, running off like that," she said. "Where've you been all this time? It's almost one o'clock."

"Here and there," he replied in the same curt voice,

getting out pajamas. It wasn't often that he didn't have to account for his whereabouts if he was out late at night and now, as the injured party, he would make the most of this too.

He gathered up his discarded shirt and under-wear — Alix had long ago trained him in neatness — and carried them into their bathroom.

Out of her sight, he sniffed his shirt for any lingering scent of perfume — he had long ago trained himself to be careful about things like that — before he dropped it with the other things into the hamper.

He could detect no scent. He had noticed that Emily's perfume had a very delicate fragrance and that she used it sparingly.

Emily. He smiled at himself triumphantly in the mirror. God, she'd been marvelous in bed and he'd got her there much sooner than he had dared to hope.

Emily. A conquest worth making and keeping. The best he'd had since Pam Baker's time.

What had become of Pam, anyway? Alix had got her out of Dunham's so fast after she found out about them that he hadn't even had a chance to say good-by to the girl. He'd been lucky not to get thrown out himself. Alix had made him crawl and beg over that episode. She had said it was his last chance.

She hadn't caught him cheating on her since. He had been too careful.

He would be even more careful over Emily. She really had got under his skin.

How soon could he manage to see her again? He'd like it to be tomorrow but he wouldn't dare plan it that soon.

Tomorrow he would have to make his peace with

Alix. He didn't want to—he couldn't bear the sight of her since this afternoon—but he would have to do it. The road to Emily lay through her.

Emily.

He hid his triumphant smile from his wife as he got into bed.

She put out the light. Nothing more was said by either of them.

10

Julie's husband had moved back into his widowed father's house when he left her. Julie called him there several times during the month of September. The fourth time he hung up on her promises of reform. The fifth time he wouldn't come to the phone, sending a message through the family housekeeper. "He says it's no use, Mrs. Graham," she reported. "He says he doesn't want to talk to you at all."

Julie made that call the last Saturday of September right after lunch. When she hung up she started drinking and drank steadily, straight shots, for the next two hours or so. Then, opening the bureau drawer to check on what was left of her private supply, her eye fell on the gun she kept locked up with it.

She took it out, instrument of oblivion . . .

Half an hour later Alix called Claude at the club and was told he was out somewhere on the golf course.

"This is an emergency," she said to the assistant

manager who had answered the phone. "Send someone out to find him and have him call me right away. He must be playing the back nine by now."

She waited beside her bedroom phone, listening to Edna out in the hall cajoling, pleading with Julie to give her the gun before she harmed herself or anyone else with it.

"Don't come near me," Julie kept saying in a thick voice as she weaved up and down the hall, occasionally coming into Alix's view as she passed her bedroom door.

After what seemed an eternity, Claude called back. "What's wrong?"

"It's Julie," Alix said under her breath. "She's terribly drunk and she's got her gun out threatening to kill herself."

"And you've been waiting around for me? Haven't you called the police?"

"Oh no. Think of the scandal!"

"Never mind about that. The important thing is to get her locked up out of harm's way."

"No, Claude, that's out of the question. You can handle it."

"All right, I'll get there fast as I can."

Alix hung up but stayed where she was. Just the sight of her made Julie worse. Edna, still pleading with her in her low rich voice, was the best hope they had.

Lock her up, Claude said. Gladly, thought Alix, if they'd only keep her. They wouldn't though. Wherever they put her, Julie, without liquor, would become a model of good behavior. They'd soon let her go and all the unpleasantness of having her put away would come to nothing.

Out in the hall Julie asked Edna to give her one good reason why she shouldn't kill herself. "Just one, Edna," she reiterated, slurring the words. "My husband doesn't want me. Nobody does. I've got nothing left to live for."

"Now, Julie, you stop that talk," said Edna in the commanding accents she had used in their childhood. "I declare, you should be ashamed, carrying on this way. You're young and pretty, you got plenty of money and a nice house, you got your sister—"

"My sister," Julie laughed scornfully. "She'd be glad to see me dead."

Yes, I would, thought Alix, and then, shocked at the thought, pressed her hand to her mouth as if she might put it into words.

"Now, Julie, don't say a thing like that about your own sister."

"But it's true, Edna. She'd be so happy to get rid of me she'd be out dancing in the streets. Come to think of it, maybe that's a reason to go on living. What a disappointment for her if I stick around, at least until I get control of my money. Because if I die before that and leave no children, then it goes to her. She and her kept husband would love to get their hands on it, wouldn't they?"

Up and down the hall Julie went, Edna only making consoling sounds now, sensing that the worst of the crisis was past.

"I'll show Alix," Julie muttered presently. "I just reckon I will. She's downstairs, isn't she?"

Julie had lost track of her sister when she slipped into her bedroom to make the phone call.

"Alix," she called. "Alix, my ever-loving sister, where you keeping your mean old self?"

Julie's voice receded as Alix stood up indecisively. She was on her way downstairs, Edna trailing her, offering to make a nice cup of tea.

"Then I'll take you back up to your room, honey, and put a nice cold cloth on your head," Edna added coaxingly.

"Oh, there you are," Julie's voice, faint in the distance, floated up the stairs. "The elegant lady having her picture painted."

She seemed to be talking to Alix's portrait in the back parlor.

A car drove up in front. Claude, Alix thought with relief, hurrying out into the hall headed for the stairs.

Halfway down she hesitated, stopped short by the bitter note that cut through the thickness in Julie's voice as she went on talking to the portrait. "Lovely lady, looking so prim and so proper—"

Edna, standing at the foot of the stairs, motioned Alix back, and the next moment shook her head at Claude as he opened the front door.

"My dear sister Alix, chatelaine of Wayland, you look as if butter wouldn't melt in your mouth but we know what you really are, don't we? You kill babies, you sweet talk Daddy into giving you control of my money—" Julie's voice rose, momentarily loud and clear. "Bitch, baby-killer, thief, that's what you are, Alix!"

Two shots echoed through the house in a sharp staccato explosion of sound.

"There," Julie cried. "There, Alix, that takes care of you."

Edna screamed. Alix clung to the banister for support. Claude stood frozen by the door.

Before they could collect themselves, Julie staggered past them through the hall and up to her room. She slammed the door after her and locked it, the click of the key loud in the silence.

"What in hell's name—?" Claude's blank gaze went from one to the other.

Edna began to weep, covering her face with her apron. Alix, ashen under her tan, said nothing. She came down the rest of the stairs and went on to the back parlor, halting in the doorway to survey the damage done to her portrait. One bullet had gone through the breast, the other through a cheekbone, looking like an obscene mole that had blossomed under the eye.

Claude came to stand beside her. "Good God," he said, and then, "She's got to be locked up after this."

Edna, coming up behind them, wept louder. "No, no, Mistuh Claude, don't even think of such a thing. Poor little Julie, it's just she's so unhappy she don't know which way to turn. All we got to worry about is getting the gun away from her. For her sake, not ours. Only person she'd ever harm with it would be her own self."

"What do you call that, Edna?" Claude pointed to the bullet holes. "Isn't that harming Miss Alix by proxy, shooting up her picture in her place?"

"Just paint and cloth, that's all it is, Mistuh Claude. Miss Julie wouldn't ever harm Miss Alix's real self. No indeed." She patted Alix's arm. "No cause to worry about a thing like that, child. Whyn't you have Mistuh Claude make you a drink? You're white as a sheet."

"Thank you, Edna, I'm all right." Alix turned to look at her. "You look pretty shaky yourself. Go sit down in the kitchen and Mister Claude will fix us all a drink."

"Miss Julie's still got that gun, though—"

"We'll think what to do about it later." Alix urged her into the kitchen and retreated to the front parlor herself, signaling Claude to bring her drink in there where they could talk in privacy.

Her face had lost its pallor but she still hadn't regained her composure when her husband came in with her drink. She took it from him, standing at a window, and then sat down.

"How Julie hates me," she said.

"Well, you're not all that devoted to her either," he countered. "There's never been much love lost between you, far as I could see." After a pause, he asked, "Shall I call the police now? They'll get that gun away from her fast and lock her up."

Alix shook her head. "No, don't call them," she said firmly. "We'll be able to get hold of the gun ourselves later. And I doubt it's as easy to get her locked up—except overnight, maybe—as you think. We'd have to get Dan down here—after all, he's her husband. He'd be the one who'd have to petition the court to commit her somewhere. There'd have to be some sort of a hearing and she'd have a right to a lawyer, wouldn't she? We don't know how she'd act or even if Dan would go along with it. It could become pretty complicated, I should think."

"I guess it could. I don't know myself if the law would say she's that bad. She gets drunk, makes scenes, but the gun is the only really serious issue." Claude paused in thought. "Maybe that's enough. Shooting holes in your picture is pretty irrational, isn't it?"

"Yes, but you heard Edna just now. She'd minimize it all she could. Julie's always been her baby, the apple of her eye. She came to us, you know, just before Julie was born."

"Yes, but it's you she's worked for all the years Julie's been gone . . ." Claude's voice fell away. Alix at five when Edna came to Wayland had probably been as self-possessed as she was now at forty and would never have been able to make a place for herself in Edna's heart as Julie had.

They went on talking about how the situation should be handled but could reach no decision on it.

"I'll have to talk it over with Spence or Roger before we do anything except get the gun away from her," Alix said at last. "They'll at least tell us what our legal position is."

Claude nodded and went out into the hall to listen at the foot of the stairs. There was no sound from above. He went upstairs and rapped lightly on Julie's door.

No answer. He turned the knob although he knew the door was locked.

"Julie?" he said. "Julie?"

A mumble, a creak of bedsprings came from the room.

She was asleep, passed out, rather, he thought, and went downstairs to report this to Alix.

They tried again at intervals. Edna tried before she went home for the night and said, "She's sleeping it off. Let her alone till morning."

In the end, that was what they did, Claude locking their door, though, when they went to bed themselves. "Just to be on the safe side," he said.

11

Julie woke up sometime in the night chilled through from sleeping on top of the bed with the windows wide open and nothing over her. She went to the bathroom, got under the bedclothes on her return and was instantly asleep again.

The next time she woke up it still seemed dark night but the first chirps outside said that the birds knew better.

She had slept well over twelve hours and was soon wide awake, aware of great thirst and a dark brown taste in her mouth. The events of yesterday came back bit by bit as she lay there bringing horror in their wake.

Dear God, what had come over her? Was she losing her mind as Dan had said more than once and Alix too? How could she face any of them again — or even face herself?

She beat her fists against the pillows in an agony of shame. How could she have acted like that — waving the gun around, shooting up Alix's picture? What was going to become of her?

Gray light coming in the window routed the dark

while Julie lay agonizing over her behavior, getting up at last to look at herself in the mirror, haunted face ghostly in that light, disheveled hair, slept-in clothes — what a sight.

Take a shower, brush her teeth, put on clean clothes — she could improve the exterior even if nothing would change the person she was inside.

She undressed, slipped on a robe and started for the bathroom, but stopped short outside her door. Claude or Alix might hear her in the shower and the last thing she wanted right now was to have to face either one of them.

But she could at least get toothbrush, toothpaste, and a towel from the bathroom and freshen up downstairs.

She went down on tiptoe, averting her eyes as she passed the door to the back parlor where Alix's picture hung. She washed up in the lavatory off the hall, brushed her teeth good and drank a large glass of juice from the refrigerator.

The sun reddened the sky as she went back upstairs and got dressed. She was ready to leave — she had no idea where she was going but the house couldn't contain her wretchedness — when she thought of the gun.

It lay on the floor by her bed. She picked it up and after giving it a long thoughtful look put it in her pocketbook. The key was in the top bureau drawer. She opened it. Yesterday's full bottle had only about one drink left in it. She would take it downstairs with her and finish it off with a little water; then take the bottle away with her so that they wouldn't find another empty around.

104

Julie locked the drawer, hung the key behind the bureau and once more hesitated before leaving the room. A note was in order after the way she had behaved yesterday or else they might have the police out looking for her.

She got paper and pen and wrote: *Woke up early, am going for a drive. Will have breakfast somewhere. Julie.* Then, after further thought: *So sorry about yesterday. It won't happen again. I'll get the picture repaired.*

She propped the note up against the mirror, picked up the bottle and went downstairs. The sun had cleared the top of the mountains by the time she left the house, red fading into yellow with the promise of a hot day to come, for all that it was the end of September. But there was still a dawn chill in the air that made her pull the sweater thrown over her shoulders closer around her when she got outside.

Julie knew what she was going to do with the gun; it would fit into her hiding place in the garage where one of the crossbeams didn't quite meet the slope of the side wall. She had discovered it in her childhood when the garage was built onto the stable and had hidden in it anything from first love letters to forbidden books in her growing-up years.

Now it would hide her gun.

The car woke Alix up. She heard it go past the house and got out of bed in time to see it vanish down the driveway, Julie's car, top down, she at the wheel.

What time was it? Half-past six. Where could Julie be going at that hour?

Alix put on robe and slippers, unlocked the bedroom door and went down the hall to her sister's room. The bedclothes were thrown back to air, the clothes Julie had worn yesterday were in a heap on the floor.

Alix's own neatness made her frown at the sight of them and go over to pick them up. The note on the bureau caught her eye. Her frown deepened as she read it. Just like Julie to be out driving around so ridiculously early on a Sunday morning. What would anyone think who saw her?

But at least she was sober and the note even included an apology.

Alix gathered up her sister's clothes and put them into the hamper in the hall bathroom. She went back to the room and emptied the overflowing ashtrays, her lips puckered fastidiously.

All that drinking and smoking. No wonder Julie was a bundle of nerves.

She tried to open the top bureau drawer. It was, as always, locked. Where was the key?

She had looked for it on several occasions when Julie first came, worrying about the gun, but this time made the most thorough search of all and found it at last when she pulled the bureau out from the wall, hanging inside the frame of the mirror.

But the drawer yielded no gun. There wasn't even a bottle. Julie had either drunk up all she had on hand or taken it with her.

Alix locked the drawer and put the key back in place. She would not tell Julie that she had found it.

It was after seven o'clock when she returned to her own room to wake up Claude. But he was already up with an early golf game scheduled.

"You'll have to cancel it," Alix said. "We're going

to search this house from top to bottom for that gun. The garage, too, if there's time before Julie gets back."

"How do we know Julie didn't take it with her?" Claude said.

"We don't. We won't know until we look."

He grumbled and complained that it was a waste of time but canceled his game. Alix went downstairs and made toast and coffee while he dressed.

Right after breakfast they began their search, a room at a time, upstairs and down, looking in every likely and unlikely place that a gun might be concealed in.

They were still searching when Julie called at noon from Brooke's to say she would have lunch there and then go to an exhibit at the Smithsonian with Spence. "Expect me when you see me," she added. "We'll probably have dinner in Washington afterward."

When they came down from the attic Alix heated a casserole Edna had left ready and then suggested searching the garage. But Julie's hiding place in the shadows up under the roof escaped their notice as it always had everyone's in the past. She herself had only found it by chance all those years ago.

"Well, I might as well have played golf for all that we accomplished here," Claude remarked when they gave up at last and went back to the house. "The gun's in her car just like I said."

"We still had to make sure," said Alix. "When she comes home one of us will have to get hold of her keys and look in her car. We've got to find it, Claude."

"Whether we do or not, call Spence about it

tomorrow. Julie's probably keeping him out of reach today on purpose. She knows you'll want to talk to him about what happened yesterday."

"Take down my picture," Alix said going into the back parlor. "I don't want anyone to see it like this. I only hope it can be repaired."

Claude eyed her grimly. "You're not showing much sense, Alix, if you're fixing to cover this thing up. It will only get worse."

"We'll see," Alix replied. "We'll talk to Spence. Or I will. She's my responsibility while she's living under my roof."

My roof, thought Claude. Not ours. Not even Julie's.

They waited for Julie to get home that night. But when she came in at nine o'clock she said she no longer had the gun.

"What'd you do with it?" Alix asked.

"Threw it in the deepest part of the river upstream from Rockwell," Julie replied. She sounded truthful. She'd had her story ready since morning.

"I'm sure you looked for it today," she continued. "Now go look in my car, Claude." She handed him the keys. "I want you both to be sure it's not there."

She looked as truthful as she sounded. She was quite sober. She said she was sorry about yesterday and that nothing like it could ever happen again now that she had thrown the gun in the river.

Claude went out to her car. The gun wasn't in it or anywhere around the garage where she might have hidden it when she drove in.

Talking it over later with Alix, neither one of them could decide whether they believed her or not.

"But at least it's out of the house and that's the main thing, isn't it?' Alix said and then added, "I'm glad you never took up hunting, Claude. I'm glad we gave away Daddy's guns when he died. I never want one in my house again."

My house. My roof. Claude glanced at her without expression and made silent additions to the list. My business. My husband. My position in the community.

Alix's position was what would count most with her where Julie was concerned, he thought, getting into bed. She wouldn't want to hurt it in any way by trying to get Julie committed somewhere for treatment. Even if Julie's husband could be brought in on it, there were people in Rockwell who would talk about Alix's control of Julie's money and her half of Wayland with its valuable land. The question of railroading her sister into a sanatorium would be raised in some quarters.

Alix wouldn't overlook that angle, you could be sure of that. Oh, she would talk to Spence but nothing would come of it. She'd find reason to object to anything he might suggest.

Which meant that they would go on putting up with Julie's antics hoping that she would eventually go back to Connecticut, or, if not there, to some other greener pasture.

Had Julie been telling the truth about throwing the gun in the river?

With her you never knew.

As Claude settled down for the night a new thought—that he should try to make love to Alix—came to him. She might refuse him, as she often did, but it must be over a week since he'd last sought her bed. It wouldn't do to have her start wondering where else he was getting his sex.

To hell with her, though, at least for tonight. He didn't feel like playing the part of my husband.

He wouldn't feel like it tomorrow night, either, come to that. He was seeing Emily. He was supposed to be going to a Chamber of Commerce meeting in Alexandria but was meeting Emily for dinner instead. They would go to her house afterward and by the time he got home he'd have no interest in his conjugal duty toward Alix.

12

It was after eleven o'clock the next night when he left Emily's.

"I don't want to leave at all," he said at the door with his arms around her, her head on his shoulder. "It gets harder every time."

"I don't want to let you go," she murmured. "But think how late it is. No Chamber of Commerce meeting lasts this late."

"Well, I'll say I went somewhere afterward with a couple of people and had a drink or two."

"Oh." Emily raised her head to look at him. He sounded very confident about what he would tell Alix. Too confident. Too—practiced.

But then, she hadn't thought she was his first extramarital venture, had she? Considering the type of woman Alix seemed to be and the opportunities a man as handsome as Claude would have put in his way, that would be too much to expect.

Even so, this train of thought made her try to draw away but Claude's arms tightened around her. "I can't let you go," he said softly. "I want you day and night. I want to marry you."

Maybe he did, at that, he thought. Maybe he really did. If Alix didn't stand in the way.

Emily tried again to draw away. "Please don't say things like that, Claude."

"Why not, when they're true? You know I love you and that we'd have a wonderful life together if Alix would let me go. I can't even begin to tell you, darling, how much you mean to me."

He couldn't have sounded more ardent or sincere. And yet . . .

What was the matter with her? Emily asked herself, when he left at last. What was the matter with her that in some corner of her mind the thought still held that they were too easy, too quick, Claude's protestations of love?

Well, did she herself really, truly love him beyond all the mixed-up feelings that had put her in her present situation?

She couldn't answer that question. She only knew that being the other woman in Claude's life was doing great damage to some part of her inner self.

Claude had found her withdrawal nothing new. Her doubts and moments of reserve were a continuing thread running through their relationship. He suspected that they would all come to a head in a crisis of one kind or another fairly soon. He tried to overcome them with talk of a divorce but how much longer would talk alone suffice?

Claude had already reached the conclusion Emily was barely facing herself; that she wasn't cut out to be any man's mistress, least of all a married man's. But while she wanted the security of marriage — assuming she believed his talk of divorce — she balked at the idea of coming between Alix and him.

In other words, Emily wanted to have her cake and eat it too.

Well, who didn't? And to give Emily credit, maybe her conscience really did bother her over Alix.

Not his, though. He was sick and tired of jumping through hoops for her and getting more kicks than favors in return.

But he was stuck with Alix as far as he could see. He hadn't saved enough money out of his salary to strike out on his own; and getting a decent job at the age of forty-five wouldn't be easy, either, unless he wanted to come far down in the world. Other companies looking for new executives would take a long look at his qualifications, coming from a family-owned business like Dunham's.

He had gone over all this many times before and never arrived at an answer that would free him from Alix. He seemed to be stuck with her until one or the other was dead. The kind of luck he had, he'd probably die ahead of her. Men usually did. Except for accidents—which Alix was too careful to have.

What would it have been called the other day if Julie had turned her gun on Alix instead of her picture? Not an accident but not murder, either, with Julie too drunk to be responsible for what she did. They'd probably call it manslaughter and shut Julie up somewhere for a few years while they tried to straighten her out.

But it hadn't happened like that. Bullet holes in Alix's picture and bullet holes in her flesh were too far apart to give them a second thought.

It would be more to the point to rehearse for Alix,

waiting for him alive and well at home, his story on what had kept him so late.

Alix could not have picked out any one incident that first aroused her suspicions of Claude. They grew out of a number of things in the next few weeks. His frequent trips to Washington with detailed explanations of why they were necessary was one of them. The lie he told her over one of those trips—that Uncle Paul had asked him to act as his substitute at a dealers convention—was another, found out about later, when Uncle Paul mentioned that Claude had offered to take his place. Then there was a complacent look—or was sleek the word for it?—that she caught on Claude's face every so often. Most of all, there was his diminishing interest in going to bed with her. It wasn't that she had ever cared much for that side of married life but she had tried to do her duty as long as Claude didn't make too many demands on her. But now, as October passed, he made almost none.

There had to be another woman, Alix thought. Emily Bartlett, never quite forgotten since the day Claude and Uncle Paul had mentioned her, came to mind. She lived somewhere in the Washington area, didn't she?

Alix had time that month to give to the problem. Julie, considerably subdued by the gun incident, was causing no trouble. When she got drunk she stayed in her room and the rest of the time was quiet and depressed.

Toward the end of October, concentrating more

114

and more on Claude, Alix found herself resorting to the time-honored devices of the suspicious wife. She looked through his pockets and bureau drawers. She sniffed his clothes thinking once or twice that she smelled perfume on them but that it was too faint to mean much, considering that there were women in and out of his office at the plant.

Finally, looking through the hamper one morning, Alix found a classic piece of evidence, a long dark hair on one of Claude's shirts. No question of its having got there through chance; it was on the inside of the shirt, caught on the shoulder seam.

Her first feeling was one of relief, almost of triumph, that at last she had something concrete to verify suspicion. Anger, iron-hard, would come later. Paying him back would come later too. She would find out more, be absolutely sure of her ground before she said a word to him about it. He'd had his last warning from her over Pam Baker and now he would have to take what was coming to him.

Meanwhile, she would keep her own counsel; he wasn't the only one who could pretend there was nothing wrong between them.

When he told her the next morning that he wouldn't be home for dinner that night and then went on to one of his elaborate explanations—an important customer, mad at their sales manager, was in Washington and Claude hoped to smooth things over by wining and dining him somewhere special—Alix said it was all right with her, that she expected to play bridge that night.

"What time are you meeting the customer?" She kept her tone casual.

"Five-thirty at the Shoreham."

"Will you be home for lunch?"

"No, I'll just grab a bite in the cafeteria."

Alix asked no more questions about his plans. Claude left, congratulating himself on how well he was handling her nowadays.

She was too restless to stay in the house after his departure. It was a crisp bright day in the last week of October, just right to work outdoors with Milton, thinning out the plants in the west border.

But first, while she was upstairs getting into an old sweater and slacks, she phoned a local car rental service. She was having some trouble with her car, she said, and if it wasn't fixed by afternoon, she would need to rent one overnight and would like to make sure there'd be one available.

"Certainly, Mrs. Whitfield," the man in charge said. "Just give us a ring. We may not have an Olds for you—"

"Any standard make car will do," Alix broke in. "As long as it's not at all flashy and has automatic transmission."

"We'll be able to take care of you," the man assured her.

Alix hung up. She went out into the yard and took Milton away from his raking to work on the border with her.

Julie, after a late breakfast, came out on the terrace with the morning paper. She said good morning listlessly but that was her usual attitude these days. It suited Alix. Since her sister insisted on staying, it was better to have her behave like that than create drunken scenes.

116

Julie's gun was never mentioned by any of them. It stayed wedged behind the crossbeam in the garage.

Brooke arrived around eleven o'clock to pick up Julie. She had persuaded her to take up golf again and they were going out to the club and would have a late lunch there after their game.

It was Edna who passed on this information. Julie hadn't bothered to. Communication between the sisters remained at minimum level since the gun incident. Alix's portrait was still at an art gallery in Washington being restored and the blank space over the fireplace was a continuing reminder of how they felt toward each other.

The rest of the morning passed. Alix read during her solitary lunch. She wasn't hungry but made herself eat the salad, rolls, and omelet Lily set before her, not knowing when or where she would have her next meal.

As she left the table she said to the maid, "Oh, Lily, please tell Edna not to plan dinner for Mr. Whitfield or me tonight. Neither one of us will be here."

"Yes, ma'am, I'll tell her." Not a flicker of interest showed on the dark face whereas Edna, acting put-upon, would ask questions. "Where you going, Miss Alix? Something sudden come up? You never said you and Mistuh Claude wouldn't be here for dinner."

At two o'clock Alix called the car rental agency again and asked to have a car delivered to her at the Rockwell Shopping Plaza at three. "I'll be out in front of Anne's Beauty Salon waiting for it," she said.

"We'll have the car there, Mrs. Whitfield. It's ready now."

"Thank you." She hung up.

She was ready to leave at quarter of three, dressed in a plain tweed suit with nothing about it to catch the eye. A dark turban hid her distinctive hair. She carried a tweed topcoat over her arm.

Downstairs she forestalled questions from Edna with a quick good-by and went out the back way to the garage.

At three o'clock, her own car out of sight at the opposite end of the plaza, she took possession of the one she was renting.

It was just what she had in mind, a gray Bel Air sedan that wouldn't draw attention from anyone, least of all Claude, who was used to associating her with her Oldsmobile.

The industrial park on the outskirts of Rockwell, convenient to I-95, provided ample parking space but Alix drove in only to assure herself that Claude's car was still parked outside Dunham's office building and then drove right out again. She couldn't miss him when he left. He would take the interstate highway and all she had to do was wait outside, pulled off the road near the main exit.

He appeared at quarter of five heading toward 95. She let his car vanish around the first curve before she set out after it.

He took 95 North, his light green Chrysler easy to follow. Alix kept her distance behind it until they got into heavier traffic as they neared Washington. Then she closed up on him and closed up still more when he blinked his direction signal for a right turn, confident that with the homegoing traffic taking up his attention, he wouldn't notice her, two cars back.

His right turn brought them to Route 7, going

west. After several miles of it, he blinked his signal for another right turn into a residential section that left all traffic behind.

This presented a problem. Alix slowed down, keeping so far behind that she almost lost him once or twice and in the end drove past the side street he took before she saw his car dwindling in the distance.

There was wooded land on either side of the street. It had a rural look until she came to a complex of townhouses and lost sight of Claude's car turning toward it.

Two signs, DEAD END and WATCH CHILDREN, were placed at the entrance road. Alix gave Claude time to reach his destination and then turned onto it herself.

It led to a court with townhouses on three sides. Claude's car was parked at the far end and she was just in time to see him being admitted to the last townhouse in the lefthand row.

So much for his appointment at the Shoreham, she thought bitterly. But hadn't she known all along that it didn't exist?

She backed her car into a vacant slot at the near end of the court and settled down to wait.

Twilight came and deepened into night. Gaslights went on in front of the townhouses. Homecoming cars began to fill up the parking area. Children playing on the sidewalks were called indoors.

What was keeping Claude all this time?

Well, she could easily guess, couldn't she?

Alix, unable to sit there any longer, got out of her car and walked down the court to the end house, stopping short in front of it. There were lights on inside but the curtains were drawn at all the windows.

119

A nameplate beside the door caught her eye. She was too far away to read it and walked up to the door, too angry to think about her own position if it opened suddenly and Claude appeared.

Mrs. G. L. Bartlett, the plate read.

Emily Bartlett. Alix felt no surprise. Her sixth sense had warned her to watch out for her from the start; Emily Bartlett, bright young widow, tramp, slut, husband stealer.

There were names for Claude too. Liar, cheat, adulterer . . .

Rage shook Alix from head to foot. She walked blindly around the corner into the welcome dark and stood flat against the building fighting for some measure of self-control.

She hadn't known such raging hatred could shake her, Alexandra Dunham Whitfield, regarded by herself and all who knew her as incapable of violent feelings. They were Julie's style, vulgar, undisciplined, inexcusable.

But at that moment she felt capable of murder. "Oh God, I could kill them both," she said through her teeth. "Especially Claude, that rotten worthless cheat, making a fool out of me like this. How dare he do it, how dare he? I'll throw him out of the house and out of his job tonight if it's the last thing I ever do. Oh God, if I only had that gun of Julie's right now—"

Her fierce whisper died away into silence as she stopped for breath and then, when it became possible, for thought.

Presently she walked around in back. The curtains there were closed, too, on all the windows.

She started back to her car but was just a short distance on the way when she heard the door of the end house open. She slipped into the shadow of a station wagon as Claude emerged with a slim dark-haired woman beside him. They were holding hands. The woman halted under one of the lights and said something that made them both laugh. Claude bent his head and kissed her.

Alix was close enough to get a good look at her face. Not really pretty, this latest fancy of Claude's. Not half of Alix's own good looks. Not even as pretty as the girl she'd got fired from Dunham's two years ago.

God knew what casual ones he had cheated with in between.

Alix retreated, keeping out of the light, as Claude opened his car door for Emily and went around in front to get behind the wheel.

Alix hurried back to her car and started the motor as they drove out of the court.

She lost them at a red light on Route 7, a neon jungle at night. It didn't matter. At seven o'clock they were going somewhere for dinner.

She stopped herself at the first snack bar she came to and ordered a sandwich and coffee. She ate as much as she could of it and went back to the townhouse, parking this time closer to Emily's door.

Claude returned at nine o'clock and went into Emily's house with her.

When they showed no signs of coming out again, Alix left. There was nothing to stay for.

She drove home, stopping at the shopping plaza to pick up her own car and leave the rented car there for the agency to call for in the morning.

She pretended to be asleep when Claude got in around midnight but lay awake long after he was asleep himself. She couldn't sleep. The tumult of her thoughts drove sleep away.

She didn't know that down the hall her sister was awake, too, crying steadily, hopelessly half the night. If Alix had heard her, she wouldn't have had to ask what was the matter. Julie, after stopping for a few weeks, had begun calling her husband again.

She had called him that evening before Alix got home and asked him to come and visit her. He said no.

Just for a few days, Dan, maybe just for a long weekend, she pleaded. I can't stand this separation. It's been nearly three months since I've seen you.

No, he said again. It's no use, Julie. We're finished. I want a divorce.

She couldn't move him. No promises from her would count after all of them that she had broken in the past.

And so they both lay awake, Alix and Julie.

Alix found some solace in putting all the blame for what had happened to her marriage on Claude. Julie, facing the wreckage she herself had made of hers, had to find what solace she could in her bottle.

13

Brooke said to her husband that same night, "I'm worried about Julie, Roger. She's so quiet these days. She's retreating from people all the time. I'd rather she got roaring drunk or something. I sort of hoped today would do some good—golf and lunch at the club and a bridge game I fixed up with Cary Moore and her visiting cousin from Georgia—but it didn't take Julie out of herself at all. I felt she was a million miles away the whole time."

"Well, I don't know what else you can do about her," Roger replied. "You can't prop her up twenty-four hours a day, can you? Seems to me you've done more than your share ever since she came back. After all, she didn't ask your advice before she messed up this last marriage—third one, isn't it, or have I lost count?"

"Third," said Brooke preoccupiedly. "Poor Julie."

"How about the poor guys she was married to?" Roger had just come downstairs from saying good night to his children and hadn't seen the paper yet. He sat down to read it and then, aware of the troubled expression on his wife's face, added, "Anyway, Alix should take more responsibility for her. Whether they get along or not doesn't change the fact that she's Julie's sister, some years older, too, and should pay more attention to her instead of letting you carry it all."

"Well . . ." Brooke hesitated as it occurred to her that in his mild way Roger might be registering a complaint over how much she had Julie around and how much of her time it took away from him.

"Maybe you've got a point," she said. "I'll have to see if I can't get it across to Alix."

"Do that," said Roger. "Don't put it off. Talk to her tomorrow."

But Alix wasn't home the next day. Lily, answering the phone, didn't know when she would return.

"She didn't say, ma'am," Lily explained. "Just that she wouldn't be home for lunch."

Brooke didn't ask to speak to Julie. She couldn't, as Roger had pointed out, prop her up twenty-four hours a day. Julie had to begin planning things for herself instead of passively accepting whatever Brooke suggested.

There was no way for Brooke, at peace with herself and her world, to even begin to comprehend the torment and desolation of Julie's.

Alix, at the moment she called her, was at a pay phone in a Northern Virginia shopping center, thinking that she would save time if she made an appointment with a detective agency before she drove into Washington. She knew nothing about them and no one that she could ask for information. When she began to look them up she was dismayed that so many of those listed had reputable-sounding names and addresses.

She recognized a few as branches of nationally known organizations but couldn't bring herself to call any of them, not knowing how large their offices were or what sort of computerized system they might have for keeping records that would put her and her problems permanently on file. They all seemed too big and impersonal, too — indiscreet. Well, not really, perhaps, she thought. But still —

She studied the services they advertised. Not specialists in tracing missing persons; not security, complete with K-9 dogs, two-way radio, twenty-four-hour protection for your home (What was the world coming to?); not armed bodyguards; not industrial espionage . . .

William Jones and Sons, Detective Agency, Domestic, Civil and Insurance Claims, caught her eye. A solid, unpretentious name, she thought, offering solid unpretentious services. The address on L Street seemed equally reassuring.

She dialed the number and was presently connected with Arthur Jones.

"Mr. Jones, I wonder if it would be possible for me to see you sometime today," she said. "It's about a — well, domestic matter."

The uncertain note in Alix's voice was familiar to Arthur Jones. Domestic matter translated into straying husband, divorce evidence, or just wanting to get the goods on him. Well-bred voice, Southern accent.

It was second nature for the detective to absorb this much about Alix as soon as she spoke. He looked at his desk calendar. "Two o'clock suit you, ma'am?"

"That would be fine."

"Your name, please?"

Her own name wouldn't do. "Alice Downes," she said. "Mrs. Richard Downes."

The uncertain note was still in her voice. False name, scared to death of what she was doing, he thought. It would be a cash retainer.

She asked directions and was told L Street between 20th and 21st.

Alix killed time with an early lunch in a department store restaurant and a little shopping. At ten minutes of two she left her car in a parking lot and walked to the address, a new office building that looked expensive enough to indicate that she had picked out no hole-in-the-wall detective agency.

The reassurance this gave Alix began to wear off in the elevator, the last of it vanishing when she found herself in the agency waiting room.

"Won't you sit down, Mrs. Downes," the competent-looking receptionist said. "I'll tell Mr. Jones you're here."

A few minutes later she ushered Alix down a short hall with frosted glass doors on either side, stopping before one lettered ARTHUR JONES.

The door stood ajar. Arthur Jones stood up to greet her, not short or tall, not dark or fair, not fat or thin.

"Mrs. Downes," he said and pulled forward an armchair facing his desk. "Do sit down."

He hadn't been prepared for anyone quite as elegant as Alix. Well-dressed, good clothes, money written all over her. Seemed as if the husband would stay home—but then, you never knew—

He made a comment or two on the weather, went

back to his desk and asked, "Now, how can I help you, Mrs. Downes?"

Alix looked at him wordlessly. What was she doing here in this sordid situation of erring husband and wronged wife about to put a detective on his trail? Even though she wouldn't mention Claude, had already thought of a way around that, it still seemed unreal that she should be here.

Arthur Jones was momentarily taken aback when she said, her voice low but firm, "I'd like some information on a woman in Falls Church."

A woman, he thought, reaching for a pad. "Her name?"

Alix hesitated. There was something irrevocable, a burning of bridges behind her, in divulging Emily Bartlett's name.

"She's a widow running her own business."

"I see." The detective kept his tone neutral but thought he did. His new client's husband was playing around with the widow.

"I'm not interested in her business activities, though," Alix continued slowly. "I'd just like to know where she goes and what she does outside of office hours."

"I see," Arthur Jones said again waiting for Alix to work up to disclosure of the widow's name.

"Just personal aspects," she repeated. "Nothing to do with—"

"But perhaps a little hard to separate, Mrs. Downes," Arthur Jones inserted smoothly. "Whoever was assigned to the investigation would have to keep an eye on the subject at work to find out who met her or where she went when she left her office."

"Oh," said Alix on a falling note. She had a sudden vivid picture of Claude meeting Emily Bartlett at her office, the two of them going out to Claude's car, laughing and holding hands as they had last night, the detective sent by the agency noting the license number and make of Claude's car and including a description of Claude himself. "Man in his early forties, six feet tall, white hair, blue eyes . . ."

Naturally the detective would do that and then find out who owned the car. He might even follow Claude home to Rockwell. Whatever he did, her own identity and the fact that Claude was her real target would be promptly discovered.

What was the matter with her that she hadn't thought of all that before she came here? How could she have been so stupid?

Alix's face flamed with embarrassment. The whole sorry business was impossible. She couldn't go on with it.

She fumbled in her pocketbook for a twenty-dollar bill, stood up and said hurriedly, "I'd better think this over some more, Mr. Jones, before I decide whether or not to go ahead with it." She laid the bill on his desk. "Will this pay for taking up your time?"

"Mrs. Downes, it's not at all necessary—you haven't been here five minutes—"

But before he could come around his desk Alix was gone from the room in full flight past the receptionist out into the corridor, wanting nothing so much as to put the scene of her humiliation behind her.

Last night it had seemed a clever plan, she thought, when she was in her car and headed for Memorial Bridge on her way home. She must have been out of her mind, though, to have even thought of going to a private detective and that she could keep her own name out of it by having Emily Bartlett followed instead of Claude.

It just went to show that when you were as upset as she had been since last night you shouldn't try to make any plans at all; you should wait until you had calmed down enough to think clearly about the whole problem.

It was only two-thirty, the traffic fairly moderate when she drove across the river and picked up 95. She would be home not long after three. No one would ever have to know where she had been or what she had done today.

She would look for a different way to handle this thing. She had never intended, anyway, to make it public knowledge in her divorce suit that her husband was unfaithful to her; she had only meant to use the detective agency's evidence of dates, times, places as a weapon against Claude, forcing him to accept her terms for a divorce without trying to fight back.

Now she would have to think of something else. Some new idea—

Or did she need one? Why couldn't she just say she had gone to a detective agency? If she followed Claude herself two or three times more as she had last night and then threw the evidence she accumulated at him, wouldn't it serve the same purpose? Claude felt so sure of himself these days, he'd be too stunned to demand proof when she said the evidence came from a private detective.

He would end up crawling to her as he had over Pam Baker. But he'd had his last chance then and there wouldn't be another. She was finished with him for good.

But even as Alix took sharp pleasure in the prospect of revenge, under it lay memories of the handsome young man who had come to Dunham's sixteen years ago and courted her with such charm and conviction that she had been able to believe that he loved her for herself alone, not for the money in back of her, as Daddy had said at first and, for all she knew, had continued to believe.

She was nearly twenty-four then and somehow, before that, no man as attractive as Claude had come into her life. She had almost been ready to settle for Mike Walker when Claude appeared on the scene.

She had really loved him in their first years together.

Now she could hardly wait to pay him back for what he had done to her . . . But still, the other feeling lay underneath.

Why did it have to end this way? It wasn't her fault. How could she have known when she married Claude that he was incapable of being true to any woman?

14

The second time Alix followed her husband in a rented car — using the same story as before with a different car rental agency — she had better luck trailing him when he took Emily out to dinner.

She parked close by when they returned and stayed on instead of going home as she had the previous week when it became obvious that they were in for the evening. She had brought along a notebook to record what went on; the time of Claude's arrival at Emily Bartlett's, the time they went out to dinner, the name of the restaurant, the time of their return from it.

She didn't leave until the hall light went on inside at twenty-five of eleven. She noted the time and then drove off to make a fast trip to Rockwell, leave the rented car at the shopping plaza and get home ahead of Claude.

He must have lingered over saying good night to Emily Bartlett, she thought. There was enough margin for her to get undressed and into bed before he came in.

As before, Alix pretended to be asleep, watching Claude from under her eyelashes as he tiptoed around the room, undressing by the light that shone in from the bathroom.

How she hated him; tonight with particular intensity for thinking he was getting away with something again. She would follow him once more to Emily Bartlett's and that would be the end.

But Julie, a few days later, precipitated a quicker end.

It was a Tuesday. She had stayed in her room most of the afternoon, coming down to dinner at the last minute. She had nothing to say at table, barely answering if spoken to and otherwise silent, drawn into herself beyond reach.

Her glazed eyes and unsteady gait had given away her condition as soon as she entered the dining room, but no comment was made on it. There was none to make. Whatever could be said had all been said long ago. Unless, Alix thought, it was to remark that Julie appeared to be drunker than at any time since the gun incident; and there would be no point in mentioning that.

But there was a sense of strain in the pretense of not noticing anything wrong with Julie; and, for Alix, the added strain of pretending that all was normal between Claude and her. It was a relief to get up from the table.

Julie went back up to her room right after dinner. She didn't want coffee, she said, when Alix suggested they have it in front of the fire in the back parlor.

Alix didn't press her. There was the theory of coffee sobering up people but it wasn't necessarily true. The best thing for Julie would be to go straight to bed, she thought, pausing in the hall to watch her sister's wavering progress up the stairs.

It was no use thinking about getting her bottle away from her either; if you found one there was sure to be another somewhere. The best you could hope for was that Julie would pass out the minute she hit her bed.

The phone rang while Claude and she were having coffee in the back parlor. He picked it up, said "Hello?" then, "Oh, hi, Paul." He listened, said, "Well, yes, but he's been with us so many years—"

Claude seemed to be on the defensive as he listened to the older man. At last he said, "You're there now? All right, I'll take a run over right away."

He hung up. "I've got to go back to the plant. Paul's still on this worrying kick about the third quarter report, volume of business down, profits down—even though he knows it's not just Dunham's. Whole economy's slowed down."

"But he seems to have some special complaint against you right now." Alix couldn't resist making the remark and then adding, "What have you done wrong this time?"

"Wrong?" Claude's face tightened. "Nothing. It's just that Paul is questioning a sixty-day extension of credit I authorized for a distributor who's hit a temporary rough spot."

He set his coffee cup aside and stood up. His flare of resentment over his wife's gibe passed as he began to think about taking advantage of this unexpected night out. "I don't know how long I'll be," he said. "You know what your uncle's like. He may want to go back twenty years in the records."

Alix's eyes followed him as he left the room. A few

133

more days and what went on at Dunham's would no longer be any concern of his.

There was bitter satisfaction in the thought. She poured herself another cup of coffee.

"Expect me when you see me," Claude said briskly from the doorway.

"Yes." Was he already thinking of sneaking in a visit to Emily Bartlett when he left the plant? Let him. It would be too complicated at this short notice to get hold of a car and follow him tonight.

She heard him drive away and picked up the evening paper trying to dismiss him from her mind.

Edna finished her work in the kitchen and came to the door to say good night. "Miss Julie in bed?" she asked.

"I hope so." There hadn't been a sound from upstairs.

Edna hesitated. "Want me to go see is she all right, Miss Alix?"

"No, I think she's better left alone."

"Well, good night then."

"Good night, Edna."

Edna left by the back door. A car door slammed outside. Milton had picked her up.

Alix finished reading the paper, got up and walked around the room. She stirred the dying fire back to life and went to the front door to look out. The sky was bright with stars. The night sounds of summer were long gone. The only sound was the rustle of dead leaves on the oaks. The air was crisp but not cold. A little walk might do her good. The house was enough to get on anyone's nerves, Julie upstairs in a drunken stupor, Claude prepared to stay out as late as

134

he dared.

She turned back for a coat, checked the door on the way out to make sure it was unlocked and went down the walk to the driveway. She would at least go as far as the bottom of the hill if not all the way to the road.

From the top of the hill she had a view of the distant lights of downtown Rockwell that could only be seen when the trees were bare of leaves. Occasional car lights passed on the road while she stood there. Otherwise, there was nothing to break a sense of being cut off from the rest of the world that was, most of the time, called privacy at Wayland.

But not tonight. Tonight it seemed more like isolation. Alix shivered in a small gust of wind, tucked her hands in her coat pockets and started off down the hill.

Julie heard her go out or rather, heard the front door close on someone, just as she had heard the earlier departures of Claude and Edna. She had been lying on her bed since dinner but the stupor Alix ascribed to her had not come. She could only fall in and out of an uneasy doze that was like a fragile shimmer of ice on a pond, barely coating the dark layers of consciousness underneath.

She turned on her bedside light finally, reached for bottle and glass and poured herself a double shot of bourbon. She drank it down, got up and stood swaying on her feet in the middle of the room, looking around vaguely as she began to wonder what she had got up for.

"For nothing," she told herself. " 'Cause there's nothing to get up for any more. Never will be, long as

I live."

She reeled over to the bureau, propped herself up against the edge and peered at her reflection in the mirror.

"Great, Julie, just great," she mumbled. "You're a wonderful girl, you are, just wonderful, the success you've made of your life." She nodded her head vigorously, lost her balance, clutched at the bureau as she fell and knocked over a lamp that shattered on the floor.

"Well, well, give the little girl a great big hand." Kneeling in the wreckage she began to cry. "Broke the nice lamp—"

But she wasn't really crying over that; drunk as she was, she knew that her tears were for the dreary wreckage of her life, all the bright promise of its beginnings as irretrievably shattered as the lamp.

Holding onto the bureau, Julie pulled herself to her feet and navigated the length of the room to the bottle.

"One more for the girl who has nothing—"

She drank and asked herself, "What was it I said before? Oh, nothing to get up for. Nothing to get up for Julie. Best thing is get rid of her . . ."

From somewhere in her mind came memory of the gun.

15

"Sticks out like a sore thumb though, these last two quarters," said Paul Dunham.

He had listened courteously to Claude's reasons for having given Manning, their Baltimore distributor, a sixty-day credit extension without first taking it up with their vice-president in charge of accounts. It was his practice to give a courteous hearing to whoever he was questioning on any problem. His dry voice did not lend itself to harsh notes; but without raising it a decibel he could, as now, make Claude feel like a jumped-up errand boy, incapable of reaching the right decision on his own.

"Manning seems to have been slipping the past two or three years," Uncle Paul continued. "Nothing to do with the current slump, all these soft spots in his sales. Been so gradual, we haven't given them the attention we should. Don't matter what story he told you about why he needed this extension or how many years he's been one of our distributors, we can't carry him on our backs much longer unless his volume improves."

"But it still seems to me that a lot of his troubles do

come from the slowdown in the economy, sir," Claude replied, respectful but insistent. "This list he showed me of his accounts due—"

"If he wants to carry his customers on his books indefinitely, that's his affair," Uncle Paul interrupted. "But we've never considered it good business practice around here. Not in the least, Claude."

He got up from his desk to end the discussion. "I'd appreciate it if you'd go over Manning's accounts several years back with Clem tomorrow. Like a report on it as soon as possible."

Claude felt like a schoolboy being dismissed after a lecture from the principal but didn't let it show as he walked out into the hall with the older man. Paul Dunham had once handled accounts himself and his disapproval of the extension of credit was giving Claude his own first doubts about it.

Jumped-up errand boy . . .

He picked up the Manning file on his way out. "Think I'll stay a while longer, now I'm here, and take another look at it," he said, wanting to redeem himself in Paul Dunham's eyes. He tried to put all of his easy charm into his smile as he added on a downcast note, "You've got me a bit worried about it, sir."

Uncle Paul couldn't help responding to the implied deference to his judgment. "Well, let's hope it's not as bad as it looks," he said opening the outside door. "Good night."

"Good night, sir."

Claude stood there until the older man got into his car and drove out of the parking lot. Then he went on to his own office and called Emily.

138

It seemed safe to use his private phone with no one around to break in on him and no pay phone nearer than the far end of the next corridor.

"Well, this is nice," she said when she heard his voice. "I didn't expect a call from you tonight."

"I'm at my office, darling. Thought I'd come back and catch up on a few things while there's some peace and quiet around here."

"Oh." Her pleasure in his call faded. He was just snatching a moment when there was no chance of getting caught at it.

But why think of that—all their moments were like that, weren't they?

"I'll be here at least another hour, maybe a little longer," Claude went on. "But then I was thinking we might have a drink together if we met at some halfway point between here and your place." He looked at his watch. "It's just past eight o'clock now. What if we make it around quarter of ten somewhere?"

"That would be fine. How about the Blue Moon on Route 1? That's just about halfway for both of us."

"Yes, it is, but—" he paused and said, "I'd rather we picked another place, Emily. The Blue Moon's quite popular with people from Rockwell. We could easily run into someone who knows me. I was thinking of a place more—well, off the beaten track."

"Why, yes, of course you were." Sudden anger put an edge in Emily's voice. "I should have thought of it myself. But I'm still not used to the sneaking around corners we have to do. What sort of dive did you have in mind for a meeting place?"

"Oh Emily, honey baby, you know I didn't mean—"

"But you did," she cut in. "What else could you have meant?"

"Well, it's just that—"

"It's just that the only place we could meet down your way is some little dive on a back road," she interrupted again on the same angry note. "Thank you kindly, Claude, but I think I'll skip it."

"Emily, honey, please don't talk like that," he said helplessly. "You know how much I love you and that I didn't mean it the way it sounded. What I wanted to say was that I've hit this trouble spot here at the office that's got me kind of worried and I thought if we could just meet at some quiet little place for an hour or so it would make me feel much better."

"No," she said. "I'm not meeting you anywhere. Good night." She hung up.

"Oh, for God's sake," Claude muttered, letting the receiver dangle from his hand.

She was good and mad at him. He'd got the whole thing screwed up. He should have named the meeting place before she got in her suggestion of the Blue Moon. She would have said yes to the place he had in mind, not a dive at all, just much smaller and more discreet.

He'd have to make his peace with her right away before she could build up a trifling thing like this into grounds for breaking off with him. With her touchy pride and the qualms she already had over their relationship, she was quite capable of it.

He didn't want anything like that to happen. He'd have a hard time finding anyone else who suited him as well as she did.

He called her back immediately.

"Please don't act like this, darling," he began. "Makes me feel terrible. Let me come and see you right now and straighten things out."

"Don't bother," Emily said. "I won't be here. I was on my way out when you called. Don't bother calling again, either, because I'm leaving the phone off the hook."

She hung up and was as good as her word. He got a busy signal when he dialed her number again.

It was a hell of a note. What should he do — give her time to cool off and then drive up to see her? No use, though, if she had gone out. He couldn't hang around her place indefinitely waiting for her to get home.

Let it go for the moment, dial her number again a little later. Meanwhile, try to concentrate on the Manning account.

Emily had been putting her coat on to go to the store for cigarettes the first time Claude called her. She was out of the house, the phone left off the hook, a minute or so after his second call.

Her anger lasted no longer than the short drive to the store. It wasn't in her to let it harden and endure. When she made the decision to break up with Claude — as she knew she would sooner or later — she didn't want to make it in anger over any such small thing as had happened tonight. Although a series of small things like it would play a part, she suspected, in her decision.

But she wasn't ready to make it yet.

Coming out of the store, she began to blame

herself for her attitude on the phone. Claude had called because he wanted to see her even if only for a little while. He hadn't been tactful over her suggestion of the Blue Moon but then, men never were about things like that. You could say they were more straightforward in their approach, more honest than women or you could say they were almost like children sometimes in their lack of tact. She hadn't been very tactful herself when she suggested the Blue Moon.

Getting into her car, Emily remembered what Claude had said about some trouble at the office and that it would make him feel better just to see her. And in return, she had been sarcastic, spiteful, and had hung up on him twice. Even now her phone was off the hook to keep him from calling her again.

She would call him the minute she got home. Or wouldn't it be better yet to drive straight to Dunham's? She could wait for him outside and follow in her car to whatever place he suggested for a drink. It would please him. He would know she really was sorry for the way she had acted.

She looked at her watch. It wasn't quite twenty after eight. At eight o'clock Claude had said he would be at his office for over an hour more. There was time to catch him before he left.

Claude made two further attempts to call Emily before eight-thirty and each time got a busy signal. Then he gave up, finding worry enough as he delved deeper into the Manning account over the extension of credit he had been so free with.

His phone rang. Emily, ready to make up and meet him somewhere, he thought hopefully, reaching for it. There was still time—he looked at his watch as he lifted the receiver—it was only ten of nine.

But it was Alix, not Emily, telling him to come right home, that Julie was on the rampage again with her gun.

"You mean she didn't throw it in the river that time?"

"Hardly, when she's waving it around upstairs threatening to kill herself."

"What phone you calling from?"

"Kitchen." Alix added in an impatient undertone, "But don't waste time on questions, Claude. Get home here as fast as you can. I'm scared to death, all alone with her."

"For God's sake, why don't you call the police—or do you want me to do it?"

"No, no, I won't have that! It's not necessary. Just get here yourself. You know you can handle her. I can't."

"All right, I'm on my way."

But when he hung up, he took the time to gather up the papers on his desk and thrust them into a drawer. Then, in what had become habit with him, he turned the cutoff key that switched his private phone over to the permanent phone at Wayland.

As he went out to his car he wondered if it wasn't a mistake not to call the police himself, regardless of what Alix said. But no, it wasn't worth the fight she'd start over it.

In his irritation at Alix—she and her goddamned worry over getting talked about—Claude shot out onto the highway, heedless of two approaching cars. The first one swerved left with a sharp blast of the horn and then swung back into the right lane in front of him.

Claude paid no attention when the second car's horn blew twice at him. To hell with that driver who hadn't been close enough to be in any danger.

He accelerated, overtook, and passed the car that had swerved around him and slowed down soon thereafter for the traffic light at the intersection ahead, the road that led to Wayland. He signaled for a left turn onto it.

It had a semi-urban look for a short stretch and then, as the houses thinned out, became a country road of fields and an occasional farm. Another mile and his lights picked up the *Wayland* sign ahead on his right. He swung up the long winding drive having left far behind the second car that had been in back of him and that had blown its horn again just past the intersection. He had no reason to think that it was directed at him. It just seemed to be a night for cars to blow their horns.

Emily, the driver of the second car, had reached the industrial park just as Claude shot out of it, narrowly avoiding a collision with the car in front of her. He was driving too fast for her to keep up and paid no attention when she blew her horn or when she blew it again after she had made the same turn at the intersection.

Then she recognized the road. He had brought her out this way after lunch the day she visited the plant last summer. His wife wasn't home, he said, pointing out the sign at the foot of the driveway; otherwise, he would have taken her up to the house.

It was hopeless trying to catch up with him. It would do no good, anyway. He had finished at the office earlier then he expected to and was now on his way home. She turned on the overhead light and looked at her watch. It was only five past nine.

Nothing for her to do but go home herself.

She came to the *Wayland* sign and backed her car around in the driveway. There were no other cars in sight. It was a quiet country road.

She caught a last glimpse of Claude's headlights at the top of the hill but could not see the house at all.

She had a letdown feeling over her fruitless trip. But she would call Claude tomorrow.

16

Alix was outside pacing up and down the brick walk when Claude stopped his car in front of the house.

"I thought I'd better get out," she said. "Julie's downstairs now with the gun and there's no picture of me to shoot at this time."

"Why didn't you just get in your car and get the hell out of here?" Claude asked without sympathy.

"Because my car keys are upstairs and I didn't want to be trapped up there trying to get them."

"Christ," he said, heading for the door. "You know you should have called the police the minute you knew she still had the gun. Must be four bullets left in it. She only fired two the other time." He looked back at Alix from the steps. "You staying out here?"

"For now. But you're in no danger from her, Claude. I'm the one she hates, not you."

He didn't answer. But the thought crossed his mind as he opened the door that Alix, putting her own safety first, didn't mind risking his. Who knew, after all, what a drunk with a loaded gun would do?

The next moment he remembered that he himself had played with the idea of being free of Alix if Julie had shot her instead of her picture that other time. So now, without knowing it, Alix was getting her own back at him.

A hell of a marriage they had, feeling that way about each other.

He closed the door behind him. He heard Julie moving around in the back parlor and went down the hall stopping in the doorway.

She was at the far side of the room staring glassy-eyed at the blank space over the fireplace where Alix's portrait had hung.

"One baby-killer down and one to go," she muttered to herself. "One baby-killer down—"

"Hi, Julie," Claude said in a matter-of-fact voice, advancing into the room. "I just got in. I've been at the office all evening and I could do with a drink. Will you join me?" He went over to the portable bar.

The gun hung from Julie's right hand. She made a fumbling effort to hide it behind her. "Don't think so." She cleared her throat as if that would clear the thickness of her speech too. "Baby-killer left—li'l old Julie—got to take care of—"

"Well, have a short one with me first," Claude got out ice and glasses and bourbon. "I don't feel like drinking alone."

He poured the drinks, making hers a stiff one, while she stood swaying on her feet, her unfocused gaze finally coming to rest on the bottle.

"Well, if you insist—"

He handed her drink to her, steered her to a chair and sat down opposite her with his own drink.

Julie couldn't get the glass to her mouth. She put the gun down in her lap to use both hands and finished off the drink without stopping for breath.

"I'll make you another," Claude said, getting up to take her glass.

"No—time—"

"Sure there is." He made her another drink, gave it to her and raised his own glass. "Bottoms up, Julie."

She barely got it down before the glass dropped from her hand and she slumped sidewise over the arm of the chair.

Claude picked up the glass, set it on a nearby table and then, watching her narrowly, reached for the gun in her lap.

It was his first chance to examine it, a Colt Cobra .32 revolver with blued barrel and walnut stock, a beautiful deadly little thing, light in weight, fitting snugly into his hand.

He spun the cylinder around. There were just two empty cartridge cases as he had expected.

He laid the gun down on the bar, went to the door and called Alix in. "It's all right," he said. "She's out cold. I doubt she'll stir before tomorrow."

Alix came in and took off her coat on her way to the back parlor. She looked first at the gun. "Did you unload it?" she asked.

"Not yet. I will."

Alix's glance shifted to her sister. Her forehead wrinkled with disgust at the sight of Julie slumped in the chair, head against the arm, a thread of saliva trickling from her open mouth onto the upholstery.

"What a disgrace," she said, her voice still tight with nervousness. "I declare, Daddy would just about die if he could see what his precious darling has come to."

She started to sit down and then stood up again.

"Make me a drink, Claude," she said. "I really need it, the scare she gave me."

He made the drink and handed it to her, noticing that she didn't say thank you. She walked around the room with it, not able to keep her eyes off Julie who had begun to snore.

"Revolting," she said, drinking faster than she usually did. "Get her upstairs, Claude."

"Give me time. Also"—his tone went dry—"there's a word called please."

"All right—please. But you don't know what this has done to me. I'm a nervous wreck over it."

"Well, it's your own fault, you and your silly pride. I told you to call the police. You should have done it, the minute you saw she still had the gun. Now it's too late. Who's to say we didn't plant it on her?"

"It doesn't matter because I have no intention of calling them, now or ever," Alix retorted sharply. "I am going to call Dan Graham tomorrow, though, and tell him to come and get Julie and have her committed somewhere up North. He's still her husband and he's got to take care of her."

"And what if he won't?" Claude demanded with equal sharpness. "He hasn't made a move so far, has he? Figures he's well out of it, if you ask me; that you're so hung up on being lady of the manor around here that you'll go right on sweeping the whole thing under the rug. But let me tell you—" The frustrations and stresses of the evening were at work in Claude, driving his temper out of control. "I'm your husband and I'm entitled to some consideration, some peace in my own house—yes, mine, too, even though you call it yours—and I'm goddamn fed up with your sister's goings-on! Just get her the hell out of here, Alix. I've had all I can take. God almighty, most husbands would have put their foot down long ago, having all their rights flouted—"

Rights. That he should dare. It was too much.

Alix, still on edge herself over the ordeal Julie had put her through, couldn't let it pass. "What rights are you talking about?" she interrupted. "You've got none left, Claude. None at all!"

"What's that supposed to mean?" He stared at her narrow-eyed.

"It should be plain enough—or shall we get Emily Bartlett to spell it out for you?" Alix's self-discipline, all her careful plans for dealing with her husband in her own time and her own way, had vanished in an instant, swept away in a burst of anger, too long suppressed.

She rushed on: "She isn't the first one you've gone tomcatting after, Claude, but she's the last as far as I'm concerned. You and I are finished. Pack your things now, tonight, and get out of this house—my house, never again yours. Clear out everything that belongs to you at the plant tomorrow. I'll call payroll and tell them to give you a month's salary in lieu of notice."

As she paused for breath, Claude tried to rally from the total shock of it to his own defense. "You've got it all wrong about Emily Bartlett and me," he began. "Sure I've seen her a few times—business appointments—working together on that computer enclosures deal—"

Alix's scornful laugh cut him short. "Were you discussing computer enclosures up in her bedroom till

151

all hours the other night?"

Oh God. She knew the whole story, no use denying it. What was he going to do, his job, everything gone. . . .

But even as his world came tumbling down, Claude's mind scuttled frantically around, seeking some plea, some approach that would at least give him breathing space, time to minimize his affair with Emily, soften Alix up enough so that he could throw himself on her mercy, beg for forgiveness as he had over Pam Baker. What had worked once would surely work again.

But first he had to make her take back her ultimatum. If she only would, he'd never go near Emily or any other woman again as long as he lived. If she only would—

"Look, Alix, you're making too much of this," he said urgently. "Please let me explain—"

"No!" she blazed at him. "Just get out. Out of this house, out of Dunham's. Go to Emily Bartlett. Tell her she can start supporting you now. God knows you're not smart enough, never have been, to get a decent job yourself."

It drove Claude into a frenzy. "You bitch," he raged at her. "You miserable bitch."

The gun was at hand. He snatched it up and shot her, the first bullet striking her below the collarbone, the second in the heart.

17

She was dead when he reached her, driven back against the sofa by the impact of the bullets, crumpling to the floor in front of it.

He couldn't believe it at first as he knelt beside her and put his arm under her shoulders to lift her up. But her head fell back and only the whites of her eyes showed.

How could she have died so quickly? There'd been only a moment or two that he'd stood there with the gun in his hand incapable of movement but then he had rushed across the room to her and as he bent over her, there'd been a funny little sound in her throat and she was dead.

He left her where she was and got to his feet, still numb with shock, staring down at her, the blood that seeped from a corner of her mouth, the wider patch of it spreading across the front of her dress.

Her lifeblood, he thought. Alix's lifeblood. He had taken her life, murdered her . . .

He backed away; not Alix any more, Alix's body.

His gaze went to Julie. Had the sound of the shots got through to her? She seemed to have changed position a little — maybe she had just slumped deeper in the chair.

He began to collect himself. There was Julie, passed out cold, Alix killed by her gun. Couldn't the two be tied together to save his own neck?

It required thought. First, though, he needed a drink, a straight shot.

He tossed it down and looked at his watch. It was just past nine-thirty.

The drink steadied his nerves. He felt able to apply himself to his situation.

He had a little leeway to plan, he thought. The night watchman at the plant had come by and spoken to him around quarter of nine. He wasn't due on his next hourly round, when he would note that Claude had left, for another fifteen minutes or so. No one working the second shift could have seen him leave before nine o'clock; the office parking lot was too far away from the factory.

There was no one on the switchboard at night; that didn't matter, anyway, because Alix had called him on his private phone.

His private phone, switched over to take incoming calls here. What a perfect alibi if he could get someone to call his office number within the next few minutes.

Who? And for what reason?

His mind clicked out the answer. Paul, whose house lay on Claude's route home.

He picked up the phone and dialed the number.

Uncle Paul answered on the second ring.

"This is Claude. I'm still here at the office, Paul, and Alix called a little while ago about her checkbook. She can't find it and says she remembers writing a check to mail on the way home when we stopped at your place the other day. She was sitting in the blue chair in your living room and thinks it might have slid down under the cushion. If it's there, she wants me to pick it up tonight. Will you take a look and call me back? I'm about ready to leave. I can finish what little has to be done yet while you're looking."

"Can't be here," Uncle Paul grumped. "Ralph would have found it. He's always cleaning things up."

"Well, just to satisfy Alix, will you take a look anyway, and call me back?"

"Women," said Uncle Paul sourly.

"I know." Claude barely managed to keep his tone casual.

"All right, I'll take a look."

"Thanks." Claude hung up and walked the floor until the phone rang, picking it up instantly.

"Not a sign of the checkbook," Uncle Paul announced. "Knew there wouldn't be. Knew Ralph cleans too good. Must be in one of Alix's other pocketbooks. Women are always changing them over. Not like Alix, though, mislaying things. She's more careful than most."

"Yes, she is, but I'll tell her where you said to look. Thanks again, Paul. Better be on my way now. See you in the morning."

"You get the figures on Manning pretty well lined up?"

Manning. Jesus, thought Claude, get off the phone. "Pretty much," he said. "Tell you about it tomorrow. Good night, Paul."

He hung up, wiped sweat off his face, and turned away from the telephone.

Nothing had changed in the room. Julie was still deep in her chair, Alix's position would never change again until someone else moved her. But the blood on her dress was beginning to dry. Wasn't there something about dried blood that indicated how long a person had been dead?

It was twenty of ten. He had to line up the time, minute by minute, from now on, the night watchman reaching his office shortly on his rounds, Claude supposedly getting a phone call from Alix right after talking to Paul and rushing home.

He should be arriving, then, within ten minutes to find Alix dead, Julie passed out with the gun in her hand—no, dropped on the floor beside her.

He had dropped it himself after he shot Alix. He picked it up—God, his fingerprints mustn't be on it—and wiped it thoroughly.

He started to put it in Julie's hand to get her fingerprints on it instead and checked himself. Hadn't he read something about tests for powder marks to show if a person had fired a gun—paraffin tests or whatever they were?

Or had he read something else that said they weren't reliable?

Well, Julie's hand had better show them, just as a precaution.

It turned out to be an awkward business to position her hand on the gun, finger on the trigger, and risky, too, in case the sound of the shot brought her out of her stupor. He steadied her arm and aimed at the sofa, pulling the trigger with his finger over hers exerting the pressure.

Julie moaned but didn't come to. He placed the gun on the floor beside her chair to look as if she had dropped it. Her glass came next, his prints wiped off, hers pressed on as with the gun.

The stage was set except for his own hands. He went across the hall to the lavatory and washed them thoroughly.

It was ten minutes of ten, about the time he should be arriving home and walking in on the death scene.

But he couldn't be expected to rush straight to the phone and call the police. He would have to get over the first shock, make sure Alix was dead, try to rouse Julie—oh, and have a drink to pull himself together.

So he had a few minutes to spare to look at his handiwork and make sure he had left nothing undone that would trip him up.

Alix's coat caught his eye; hang it in the closet so as not to suggest that she had ever left the house.

He moved back to the door to study the scene and review the story he would tell the police.

He would say Alix had called him around twenty minutes to ten—the time was close, right after he had talked with Paul, but Julie could have shot her as soon as she hung up the phone. She had fired three shots, counting the one into the sofa, a wild shot they would expect, considering how drunk she was.

Claude's glance settled on her, the patsy, the sitting duck . . .

But nothing much would happen to her over this, he assured himself. People who knew her would vouch for her history of drinking, past and present. Then there was Edna to bear witness to the hostility

157

between Alix and Julie and the climax it came to that other time when Julie got drunk and shot at Alix's picture.

It all added up to so much evidence pointing to Julie that the police would have no reason to doubt her guilt. But it wouldn't be the guilt of murder in her case as it would be for him. Julie, drunk, couldn't be held accountable for her own actions. She would just be put somewhere — as she should have been already — for treatment.

No one would hold Alix's death against her when she was released — because who could say what they'd do themselves if they were dead drunk? It could almost be looked at like a drunken driver killing someone on a highway.

Even for himself, it could be looked at like that. God knew, he hadn't meant to kill Alix. It was the things she had said —

Claude hesitated as he started for the phone to call the police. Her checkbook. It had to be missing, more or less, to cover his phone call to Paul.

He hurried upstairs, hunted through her pocketbooks for it and then looked around the room for a place to put it. The chaise lounge was the nearest thing to the chair she had sat in at her uncle's. Probably no questions would ever be asked about it, he thought, as he shoved it down behind the cushion, but it was better to leave no loose ends.

He went back downstairs and called the police.

18

Claude had a few minutes to himself, a grace period, before anyone from the police could arrive. Was there any particular action that he might be expected to take during those few minutes, a man coming home to find his wife's body on the floor, his sister-in-law passed out in a chair with a gun beside her?

Yes, he thought. Call someone, seek support from some close friend or member of the family.

Spence Hollis? No. Getting a lawyer on the scene immediately, even as a friend, wasn't a good idea.

Paul would have to be called but not yet. The alibi he would give Claude could wait. It looked better that way than hurrying to produce it.

Brooke, of course. As Julie's closest friend it would be only natural to ask her to take care of her. She would tell Roger what had happened before she came rushing over and he would then call Spence. If Spence turned up here after that, it would be on his own initiative, not because Claude had called him right away.

Maybe, Claude thought while he was dialing the

Parkers' number, he was bending over backward with all this involved thinking, but it was better to be safe than sorry.

Brooke answered the phone. She exclaimed with horror when Claude told her he had got home from his office a few minutes ago and found Alix dead on the floor. "Oh no," she said. "It can't be true."

"I'm afraid it is," he replied. "Looks like bullet wounds, although I haven't moved her or anything. She called me at the plant — I'd gone back after dinner — and said that Julie was drunk and had her gun out. I came right home —"

"Where's Julie now?" Brooke interrupted.

"Passed out cold. I couldn't wake her up when I got in. The gun is on the floor beside her."

"Oh God." Brooke gave a quick gasp for breath.

"I've called the police," Claude continued. "They're due any minute but I wondered, seeing how close you and Julie are, if you'd —"

"I'll be right over," said Brooke, and hung up.

As Claude hung up himself, he thought of Paul Dunham again. It would look funny if he didn't call him soon, Alix and Julie's closest kin.

But still he hesitated. Overshadowing his reluctance to produce his alibi immediately was the more important matter of too many phone calls made in too fast a sequence to suit him. First there was the alleged call from Alix about her checkbook that indicated nothing was wrong here at the time. Then came his call to Paul and Paul's calling him back. Right after those two calls, he would have to say, Alix had called again to tell him about Julie.

But wait — he hadn't told Paul that Alix had just

that minute called about her checkbook. He could say that he was busy at the moment and let fifteen or twenty minutes go by before he got around to calling him about it.

That would help some. Even so, he would wait a little longer to get in touch with Paul in the hope that the time sequence of his call to Claude and the second one from Alix, that she was supposed to have made right after it, would be less clear in his mind.

But Claude, as he turned away from the phone, was jarred by the sudden realization that he should never have mentioned Alix's call about Julie at all. There was no need of it. All he should have said was that he got home at ten o'clock after working late at the office. That would have been the end of it, avoiding the whole tricky business of what time the various calls were made.

Now it was too late to change his story. He had told it to Brooke. He had been too smart for his own good, thinking that the safest thing was to stick as close to the truth as possible.

He heard a car outside and then the doorbell. He took a deep breath before he went to answer it, shaken by the realization that he had already made one mistake in what had seemed like a foolproof plan to make Julie the scapegoat in Alix's death.

Were there other mistakes too? It was all happening so fast, he didn't have time to weigh his every word and move.

But even if he had more time, he thought, opening the door, how could he be expected to be letter-perfect in getting away with murder? He had never killed anyone before. He hadn't meant to kill Alix.

161

And was he wholly to blame for that when he'd had her razor-sharp tongue slashing at him until it drove him into temporary insanity?

A uniformed young officer stood on the porch, vaguely familiar to Claude as a member of the police force although he didn't know his name.

The officer knew his. "I'm Patrolman Stapleton, Mr. Whitfield," he said. "I understand there was some trouble here—?"

"Yes, Officer," Claude said, stepping aside to let him in. "My wife. She's down the hall."

He led the way to the back parlor.

Stapleton went into the room, bent over Alix, paused in front of Julie, limp in the chair, to eye her closely. He looked at the gun on the floor beside her but did not touch it.

He did not, in fact, touch anything. He even walked lightly as if a heavier tread might disturb some part of the pattern. His glance came to rest on the telephone. He could have gone out to the cruiser to make a radio report to headquarters but he had been taught at the training school in Richmond that only under emergency conditions should an officer leave the scene of a violent death before assistance arrived.

"May I use your phone, sir?" he asked over his shoulder.

"Certainly," Claude said from the doorway. It was the first word he had spoken since admitting the young man. He had made one mistake already, talking to Brooke, and would not make another, volunteering information to this underling who was first on the scene.

162

He even made it a point to withdraw into the hall as Stapleton, his handkerchief wrapped around the receiver, picked it up and dialed the police station. His show of tact didn't matter; from what he could hear of the conversation as he walked up and down the hall, the officer was using some sort of code words.

After he hung up, Claude still said nothing until it occurred to him that it was an omission on his part not to have called Hatfield, the family doctor. That was the natural thing for a man walking in on his wife's murdered body to have done, wasn't it, even though she was plainly beyond medical help?

"I was just going to call our family doctor when you arrived, Officer," he said. "His line was busy when I tried before. Shouldn't I call him now?"

"That won't be necessary, sir. There's nothing he could do for Mrs. Whitfield and the medical examiner will be here soon."

For all its politeness, Stapleton's tone was as noncommittal as his expression. He was on guard at what looked like a murder scene, apparently relaxed as he stood in front of the fireplace but taking nothing for granted.

He asked no questions, though, leaving all that to his superiors. But the silent waiting for their arrival was too much for Claude. He went back into the room and shook his head mournfully looking down at Alix.

"I still can't believe it," he said, "coming home from working late and finding my poor wife—"

Stapleton made some sound that might have been meant to convey sympathy.

It was a relief to hear a car drive up. Running

footsteps on the porch told Claude it was Brooke. He hurried to admit her, the officer following him out into the hall.

She put her arms around him for a moment. "Oh Brooke," he said. Then came introductions. "This is Officer Stapleton . . . Mrs. Parker, an old family friend, the first person I called after the police."

Brooke nodded—she knew Stapleton—and turned back to Claude. "Where's Julie?"

"Down the hall."

Brooke rushed to the door of the back parlor, stopped short. "Oh dear—"

"Be better, ma'am, if you don't go in there yet," Stapleton said.

"But if you'll just let me try to wake her—" She broke off as her distressed glance fell on the gun. She was a lawyer's wife, aware of restrictions at a scene like this. She turned back to Claude. "Is everything the way it was when you got home?"

"Yes."

"But how long do you think—"

Stapleton interrupted, keeping his tone courteous. "Why don't you and Mr. Whitfield sit down in the other room, Mrs. Parker?"

"In a moment." Her gaze was still on Claude. "Have you called Uncle Paul?"

"My God, no." He clapped his hand to his head. "I forgot him, the state I was in."

"Well, don't wait another minute."

"If you'll both just sit down for now, Mrs. Parker," said Stapleton.

Brooke shook her head. "Mr. Paul Dunham, Mrs. Whitfield's uncle, must be notified right away. Mr.

164

Whitfield should make the call."

Stapleton surrendered. "Is there another phone you could use, sir?"

"Yes, Officer." Claude headed for the kitchen.

Uncle Paul had gone to bed. There was no way to soften the news but he took it well. He said he would come over as soon as he got dressed.

More police arrived while Claude was on the phone to him. There was a plainclothesman in charge who introduced himself as Lieutenant Conrad; also a photographer and two men with lab equipment. (Claude wondered if they had brought wax for a paraffin test of Julie's hand but had no way to find out that they thought the test of too little value to use it.)

Claude and Brooke were relegated to the front parlor with the double doors between the two rooms closed. Stapleton was sent back on patrol, another officer appearing in his stead. The next arrival was the medical examiner who nodded to them on his way through the hall. A few minutes later a middle-aged woman came in, a police matron, they would find out later, although she was not in uniform.

Presently Claude was asked which room was Julie's and then there were sounds that indicated she was being carried upstairs.

Uncle Paul drove up and had to have his identity verified before he was admitted by Stapleton's replacement who seemed to be in charge of the front door.

They sat and talked, the three of them, in low voices, Claude taking his time over questions, measuring every word he said.

165

At last Lieutenant Conrad came in from the hall followed by another officer. Claude started to introduce him to Uncle Paul but the latter was too prominent a figure in Rockwell to need an introduction.

Conrad shook hands with him and expressed sympathy as he had to Claude when he first arrived. Brooke asked how Julie was. Still unconscious upstairs in her room under the police matron's care, Conrad said, and added that Brooke was free to go upstairs and join them.

He sat down when she was gone, his subordinate beside him taking out notebook and pencil. "Now, Mr. Whitfield, will you tell us whatever you can about this, right from the beginning," he said.

Claude had Paul Dunham there to verify the way it began, their get-together at the office after dinner to discuss an account, the older man's departure around eight o'clock — "About that time, wasn't it, Paul?" — Claude's decision to stay on at his desk to go over some more figures on the account . . .

Impeccable, so far, not a flaw anywhere — how could there be when it was all perfectly true? — but thereafter it became trickier, watch every word —

"Sometime later on — I wasn't keeping track of the time but it was nine o'clock or so — my wife called me. She said she couldn't find her checkbook and that the last time she remembered using it was when we were at Mr. Dunham's two or three days ago. It might have slipped down behind the chair cushion, she thought, and if it was there, she wanted me to stop and pick it up on my way home."

Conrad turned to Uncle Paul. "But she didn't call

166

you herself, sir, to ask about it?"

"No, she didn't." Uncle Paul paused, then added, a wonderful piece of luck, thought Claude, "I was on the phone myself, though, around that time. She might have tried my number and got a busy signal."

Claude didn't try to emphasize the point. "She made no mention of that to me, sir," he said. "She just asked me to call you because I'd be the one to stop by if the checkbook was at your place."

"Was Mr. Dunham's line still busy when you called him?" Conrad inquired of Claude.

Was the damn fox already checking up on the time sequence? "No, I got him first try," Claude replied. "But that wasn't right away. I didn't get around to making the call until I was almost ready to go home. That was — well, what time would you say it was, sir?" He made a show of consulting Uncle Paul.

The older man shrugged. "Didn't notice. Must have been about nine-thirty or maybe a bit later."

Thank God he wasn't pinpointing it any closer than that, Claude thought.

"Did you talk very long?" the lieutenant asked, directing the question at Claude.

"Only long enough to tell him why I was calling," Claude replied. "I was sorting papers and asked him to look for the checkbook and call me back."

"How is your switchboard handled at night, Mr. Whitfield?"

"It's connected direct after the office closes at five o'clock. But I have a private phone and Mr. Dunham called me back on that." Claude's voice quickened to carry them past the ticklish moment when Uncle Paul might make some comment on the way calls could be switched over from the office to the house. "He said the checkbook wasn't there and that with all the pocketbooks women have, my wife had probably put it in a different one."

"That's right," Uncle Paul said, his attention diverted from telephones to feminine foibles. "Lot of nonsense, changing pocketbooks every time they change their dress."

Conrad smiled but immediately turned the conversation from women's accessories back to murder. "How soon after Mr. Whitfield called you did you call him back, Mr. Dunham?" he asked.

"Oh, three or four minutes, maybe. Or not that long. Just long enough to look under the cushion of the chair and see that the checkbook wasn't there."

"So if we say you called back no later than twenty minutes to ten, say, that's about right?"

"Pretty close."

The lieutenant shifted his attention to Claude. "How soon after that did Mrs. Whitfield call you to come home?"

"Almost immediately."

"Making it around twenty of ten, not much more than half an hour after she called you about the checkbook." Conrad looked thoughtful. "The thing certainly blew up fast, considering that she made no mention of her sister's condition or the gun that first time."

Christ, if he only hadn't mentioned them himself, Claude thought as he replied, "At that time my sister-in-law must have still been in her room and my wife couldn't have known she had the gun. As soon as things got bad, she called me to come home."

He went on to stress Alix's statement that Julie was threatening to kill herself and then ventured an opinion designed to help her. "Alix may have tried to get the gun away from her and in the struggle it went off —"

A shade of relief crossed Paul Dunham's face quickly removed by Conrad who said, "Under different circumstances, yes. But according to Dr. Douglas's preliminary examination, neither of the two bullets that struck your wife was fired at close range, to say nothing of a contact wound such as might occur in a struggle for the gun. Also, there seems to have been a third shot that went through the back of the sofa."

"Oh," said Claude.

"There are still two bullets unaccounted for," Conrad continued. "One is still in the chamber. Do you know anything about the other two? In fact" — he settled back, his fleshy face without expression — "best thing would be for you to tell me whatever you know about the gun; where your sister-in-law got it and when; and if she brought it with her, was it loaded or did she buy the ammo here in Virginia where she'd have to sign for it. Also" — his tone hardened a little — "how long ago you and Mrs. Whitfield found out she had the gun and why you allowed her to keep it, in view of what Dr. Douglas, who has some acquaintance with her, was able to tell me about her drinking habits."

Claude listened to the police lieutenant with a sinking feeling. He hadn't thought about the distance the bullets were fired from ruling out an accidental shooting. That suggestion hadn't helped Julie and now he would have to tell the whole history of the gun and let Julie look after herself.

He began with Julie's arrival with the gun in her car three months ago—Milton would verify that—and her insistence on keeping it locked up in her room. Then there was Edna coming into the story as a witness to the drunken shots fired at Alix's picture which was still, he explained, at the dealer's in Washington.

Paul Dunham bristled. "Nobody told me a word of this, Claude. I had a right to be told—my own nieces, my brother's daughters."

His sputters died away under Conrad's stare, his coldly polite, "If you wouldn't mind, sir, going into the family side of it later?"

Claude went on to Julie's story of throwing the gun in the river the day after the shooting incident. "We weren't sure of it, of course, but what could we do, Lieutenant? We searched the house from top to bottom without finding it. Wherever it was hidden, it wasn't under this roof. So in the end, we were inclined to believe her . . ."

Conrad made no comment. He asked directions to the tenant house and sent for Edna and Milton.

Spence Hollis arrived. His status, lawyer or family friend, seemed uncertain at first but then, while the lieutenant and his subordinate were out of the room for a few minutes, Uncle Paul spoke up.

"Spence, as Julie's uncle I'm retaining you to represent her interests. Looks like the worst fix she's ever got into and I want you present when she's fit to be questioned."

"She has the right to her own choice of counsel,"

170

Spence pointed out. "I'd have no standing unless she—"

"Just for the time being," Uncle Paul interrupted. "The way it looks, she mustn't answer any questions whatsoever without your approval."

"Yes, sir," Spence said gravely, his tone reflecting agreement that Julie was in the worst fix of her life.

Claude had a sinking feeling again. It couldn't be as bad as Paul and Spence and the lieutenant made it sound. Julie was dead drunk. How could anyone in her condition be held responsible for what they did?

19

But the law, Claude soon learned, took a different point of view. Conrad talked of taking Julie to jail that night or at least to the emergency room of the hospital for sobering up.

Dr. Hatfield was called in. His statement that the only treatment Julie required was time to sleep off her drunk had the support of Dr. Douglas, the police doctor.

Spence then used all his powers of persuasion to have Julie left undisturbed for the night, pointing out that it hadn't been established yet that Alix had been killed by bullets from Julie's gun or what circumstances had led to her death.

Conrad finally agreed that Julie could remain where she was with the police matron staying in her room with her.

There was little sleep at Wayland that night for anyone but Julie. Edna and Milton were questioned separately in the kitchen. They gave reluctant support to Claude's story on the gun and were taken home, Edna in tears over being refused permission to look after Julie. Alix's body was removed for autopsy. The police were gone by one-thirty, leaving an officer on duty in the hall outside the sealed-up murder room that would be re-examined in the morning.

Uncle Paul, face gray with fatigue, made his departure, suggesting to Claude that they postpone calling Julie's husband until she was able to tell her story. Spence Hollis left at the same time, having arranged that Brooke would call him the moment Julie woke up.

Brooke retired to the guest room in front. The police matron dozed in an armchair in Julie's room.

Claude went to bed and fell into a fitful sleep around three o'clock, waking up at six to worry about the day that lay ahead.

What Julie would say, what she would be able to dredge up out of her subconscious, loomed large in his mind. But he had other worries, too, bleakest at this hour with the house silent around him. There was the remote chance that the night watchman at the plant might have arrived early at Claude's office on his rounds and be in a position to destroy Claude's alibi with the first question the police asked him. There was the much greater chance that Claude's secretary might try to use his private phone or just happen to notice that he had turned the cutoff key on it.

That worry was one he could eliminate, he thought, looking out the window at the first subtle changes that heralded dawn. All he needed was some excuse for taking a run over to his office now—

The Manning file, of course.

He was out of bed in a moment, turning on the bathroom light for a quick wash and shave, getting dressed and going quietly downstairs.

He had a story ready for the policeman on duty in the hall. He couldn't sleep, he said, and had just thought of some papers he wanted to straighten out at his office; it would only take a few minutes.

"Yes, sir." The officer would report Claude's departure from the house and the reason he gave for it but had no orders to prevent it.

Claude had his own key to a side door of the office building. He left his car in the parking lot, the only one there at that hour, in contrast to a steady stream going into the parking lot next to the factory.

He let himself in and went looking for the night watchman who would go off duty at seven o'clock. He found him in the corridor leading to his own office and stopped to speak to him.

The man didn't know about Alix. The police hadn't questioned him yet. They might not question him at all, Claude thought relievedly, considering how well-established his alibi must seem to them.

The watchman expressed shock and sympathy. "What time did it happen, Mr. Whitfield?" he asked.

The crucial question. "Before ten. Before I got home."

"Oh yes. I remember noticing you'd gone, sir, when I got to your office around that time."

One worry laid to rest. Switching back his private phone took care of another. He put the Manning file together—the last thing he cared about at the moment—and left a note for his secretary to attend to it.

Two worries laid to rest, he thought, driving out of the parking lot. He could do nothing about his major one, Julie, what she might or might not be able to remember, but at least no one would ever be able to prove now that he wasn't at his desk, a ten-minute drive from Wayland when Alix was shot there last night.

His thoughts turned to Emily on the way home; first, that she would expect him to call her sometime today even if she had already heard about Alix's death from some other source; then, with a twinge of anxiety, he thought of the two calls he had made to her from his office last night, toll calls, that were now on record at the phone company.

A moment's reflection brought reassurance. If they ever came to light, he could always say an idea had popped into his head for a new survey on computer enclosures and he hadn't waited to call her at work today in case he couldn't reach her.

Everyone at the office knew about their previous association. And at home even Julie must have some recollection of his mentioning Emily's name to Alix in connection with the survey. Alix had certainly become familiar with it at the time.

Not just at the time either. Good God, what was the matter with him that he hadn't asked himself before this how she'd found out about his affair with Emily?

Claude pulled over to the side of the road and lit a cigarette.

How had she found out—a private detective? Jesus, was it that, with the man already having sent in a report that was somewhere among her papers?

Get home and look for it ahead of the police who might ask to go through her desk.

But what good would it do if there was one and he

176

destroyed it? The detective would have his own copy of it as well as information carried around in his head.

If Alix had hired one her checkbook might show who it was. Once he had the name he could think about trying to buy him off.

It was almost seven when Claude got back to Wayland, spoke to the officer again and went upstairs.

He heard stirrings on the way, a murmur of voices from Julie's room. The door to the front guest room stood open. Brooke had gone in to see Julie.

He listened in the hall but couldn't hear what they were saying. Whatever it was, he had no control over it and had a more immediate concern at the moment.

His door shut, he took Alix's checkbook out from under the cushion and went through the check register for the past three months. It showed all the usual entries recorded in Alix's neat handwriting, including checks made out to cash, but none excessively large to suggest a sizable retainer paid out to a private detective or additional fees paid later.

Claude felt both relieved and puzzled. What other way could Alix have found out about his affair with Emily? It didn't seem possible that she could have followed him herself without his noticing her car but she just might have managed it. Or else, suspicious of his trips to Washington, she had got hold of Emily's home address and kept watch from somewhere in the court.

The morning's mail was to relieve Claude's mind completely. It would include a bill from the car rental agency Alix had used at the end of October.

177

Julie had waked up a little earlier. She tried to sit up and fell back with a groan. The next moment a middle-aged woman she had never seen before bent over her.

"Mrs. Graham?" she said.

Julie eyed her groggily. "Who're you and what are you doing in my room?"

"I'm Police Matron Reynolds," the woman replied. She picked up the phone beside the bed and dialed a number—it was police headquarters—holding the phone to one side, her head turned away from Julie as she spoke into it briefly.

Julie wasn't listening. She struggled to sit up holding her head in her hands. "What's going on here?" she asked. "What's it all about?"

"Just a minute, Mrs. Graham. I'll get Mrs. Parker."

"Brooke is here?" Julie stared at her as she went out into the hall and rapped on the guest-room door. A moment later she returned, followed shortly by Brooke wearing one of Julie's robes.

"Brooke—what on earth—?"

"There's been some bad trouble, honey," Brooke said. "I'm not supposed to talk about it. The police will be here before long. Meanwhile, you take a shower and get dressed and I'll run down and make some coffee. Mrs. Reynolds will be here if you need help." She paused at the door. "I'll call Spence now. He'll be right over."

"Spence—you mean I need a lawyer?"

Brooke, silenced by a glance from the police matron, made no reply. She left Julie alone with the woman who would give out no information at all.

A half hour later Julie was downstairs, pale and

shaky but fortified by a shower, aspirin taken with a large glass of water, fruit juice, and black coffee. She was wearing a sweater and skirt and had put on a little make-up.

When she saw the police officer stationed outside the back parlor she again demanded to know what was going on.

Brooke had gone upstairs to dress. Claude came down to get a cup of coffee.

"Where's Alix?" Julie said but he only looked at her uneasily and went away.

Lieutenant Conrad arrived. He came into the front parlor where she sat with the police matron, closed the door and introduced himself to Julie, thinking how different she looked from the sodden drunk he had seen last night.

His glance, cold and impersonal, frightened her. "What's happened here?" she asked. "Where's my sister? Her husband won't say."

"Your sister is dead," Conrad replied in a flat voice. "She was shot to death in the next room last night."

"What?" Julie cried. She was standing up when he delivered the blow. Her legs wouldn't support her. She sat down on the nearest chair and looked at the bulky graying lieutenant in total disbelief. "Alix dead—shot to death—oh, my God—" She tried to collect herself, hands gripped in her lap. "Who did it? How did it happen?"

"That's what we're trying to find out, ma'am," said Conrad. "You seem to have been the only other person in the house at the time and we hope you'll be able to help us. Before I ask you any questions, however"—his voice took on a formal note—"I must first advise you that anything you say can be used against you in a court of law and that it is your constitutional right to refuse to answer any questions or make any statement whatsoever or if you so choose, to have an attorney present during this interrogation."

Julie stared at him. "You think I—? Oh no! Never, never." She shook her head so vehemently that it started to throb again and then pressed her hands against it to ease the sudden pain.

The matron went out and came back with a glass of water.

"Was there someone else here last night, Mrs. Graham?"

Julie gave him a helpless look and said, "I don't remember. Oh God, you really think I did it, don't you? All that talk about my constitutional rights . . . Get Spence Hollis. Get him now. I won't say another word until you do."

Spence Hollis, as if on cue, drove up just then and was shown into the room by an officer who remained to take notes. Spence's presence steadied Julie. She would answer whatever questions he approved of, she said.

Yes, she owned a Colt Cobra .32 revolver. Yes, she would look at the one found beside her chair last night. Yes, it was either her gun or twin to it. Yes—with Spence's reluctant assent after Conrad made it plain that it was a choice between here and now or taking her to headquarters—she would allow her fingerprints to be taken.

The fingerprint man was brought in. Conrad took

advantage of the interval to turn over the gun and the bullets that had killed Alix to an officer waiting outside. He would hand-carry them to the ballistics section of the FBI in Washington and request an early report on their findings.

When the fingerprinting was over, Conrad went back to questions about the gun. Where had she bought it? Connecticut, several years ago, when she was living alone for a time. The ammunition? No, not bought in Virginia but in Connecticut. No, she'd had no permit to transport it from Connecticut to Virginia in her car, or known that she needed one.

Yes, she remembered getting the gun out last night after drinking in her room until she was very drunk. There were lights on in the house, upstairs and down, but no sign of Alix when she slipped out the back door to the garage where she had hidden the gun.

She described the hiding place. An instant check revealed it empty.

"Of course," she said. "I just told you I went and got it, didn't I?"

There was still no sign of Alix when she returned to the house but a few minutes later she heard the front door open and close and assumed it was her sister coming in. No, she didn't know where she had been.

Back in her room, Julie continued, she had another drink or two and had a hazy memory of walking around with the gun in her hand.

"What was your reason for getting it out of the garage?" Conrad asked.

"You needn't answer that question, Julie," Spence inserted but she shrugged off the warning, a stark looking coming to her face.

181

"I intended to kill myself," she said.

The lieutenant hesitated. "May I ask why, ma'am?"

She met his gaze stonily. "Because I've made a mess of my life. Because every day there's less and less to live for."

A silence followed this statement of defeat. Conrad, after a moment, said, "But then you left your room, didn't you?"

"Yes. I thought—no, I can't say that because I was past being able to think—I felt that the walls were closing in like—well, like a coffin, I guess—that I'd rather go outdoors to carry out what I intended to do." She paused. "I'm not sure what I did next—wandered from one room to another, I think. But I could hardly walk by that time. I don't know how I got downstairs. I don't remember seeing my sister at all—and yet it seems that at some point she was standing in the hall near this room—maybe she said something—because I think I fell part way downstairs . . ."

Claude, who was on the phone in his bedroom, making arrangements with an undertaker to take charge of Alix's body as soon as it was released to him, would have had his greatest worry eased if he could have listened to Julie's halting account of what had happened last night.

Conrad could get no more out of her. Everything that had taken place from the time she fell downstairs until she passed out was gone from her, although she would have given Claude a bad moment if he could have heard her ask, "Didn't my brother-in-law come home, though?"

"Yes, but not until it was all over."

"Oh." Julie let it go, the hazy recollection that had flickered in and out of some recess in her memory.

Spence tried to help her. "Think, Julie," he urged. "You were in the back parlor with Alix. She must have asked you to give her the gun—"

"Mr. Hollis," Conrad said dryly.

The best Julie could do was to tell them she remembered voices and people around her at some point—or maybe it was just part of a dream she thought she'd had.

Spence sighed. She had moved ahead to police activity. The crucial interval of Alix's death remained blank.

Spence would not let her answer any questions on the gun incident involving Alix's picture; or on what kind of a relationship she'd had with her sister except to state that they hadn't seen much of each other in recent years and were not very close.

Eventually it was over, Conrad repairing to the back parlor to see what progress was being made in the examination of the room by daylight. Nothing new, he was told, had turned up so far.

Edna brought breakfast trays to Julie and Spence and the police matron. Brooke joined them, coaxing Julie to eat but all she wanted was a glass of milk.

While Conrad was in the back parlor the fingerprint man called him to report that a partial print found on the trigger of the gun and a thumbprint on the stock matched Julie's.

That, on top of all the other evidence he had, about wrapped it up, Conrad said.

He took Julie to headquarters and then before a magistrate on the charge of murder. Arraignment in municipal court was set for the following week.

Spence talked with the Commonwealth's Attorney but he wouldn't hear of bail. After a long discussion of Julie's drinking and related problems he agreed to get a court order to send her to Central State Hospital in Petersburg for psychiatric examination.

Later that day, Paul Dunham called Julie's husband who said he would arrive in Rockwell early the next morning.

20

Emily heard about Alix's death on a seven-thirty news broadcast that morning. The radio she'd had since college stood on the counter by the kitchen sink. She turned it on every morning when she came downstairs to start breakfast as automatically as she plugged in the electric percolator.

The brief mention of Alix came after national and international news. *"A forty-year-old Rockwell woman was found shot to death in her home late last night . . ."*

Rockwell. The name brought Emily to startled attention in the middle of the kitchen.

"The body of Mrs. Alexandra Whitfield was discovered by her husband, Claude Whitfield, on his return from work late last night. Mrs. Julie Graham, sister of the dead woman, staying at the family home, was found unconscious in the same room.

"Mrs. Whitfield was the daughter of the late Horace Dunham, prominent Rockwell businessman and civic leader and the granddaughter of the late James Dunham, founder of the Dunham Office Furniture Company.

"A police investigation is under way but no theories have been advanced as yet."

Emily sat down on the nearest chair looking dazedly at the dish she had just taken out of the cupboard. Alix Whitfield dead, shot to death. Murdered. Her sister Julie found unconscious—what did that mean?—in the same room. Found by Claude—

Bright cheery music followed the news. It grated on Emily, bringing her to her feet to turn it off.

The coffee was perked, the toast popped up. The poached egg she had forgotten was leathery in the pan. She put it in the disposal and sat down at the table with coffee and toast.

Her mind had begun to function again. Julie drunk, taking pot shots at Alix's picture that other time; Julie found unconscious in the murder room last night; wasn't that another way of saying Julie found drunk?

She had killed Alix. Things Claude had said about the enmity between the sisters had pointed toward the terrible climax that had been building up, it now seemed, since Julie's arrival months ago.

Claude had found them. He had been rushing home last night when she had just missed him at the plant.

Rushing home as if he knew. Could someone have called him? No, of course not, when he was the first one to walk in on the scene. Then why had he been in such a hurry?

Emily puzzled over this question until she remembered what Claude had told her about Alix calling him to come home and cope with Julie the other time she had her gun out. She must have called him last night too. But last night he was too late.

Had Alix tried to get the gun away herself and been killed in a struggle over it or had Julie shot her deliberately?

186

Apparently that question hadn't been answered yet.

Emily's toast, cold on the plate, followed the egg down the disposal. She turned on the eight o'clock news while she had another cup of coffee but the report on Alix's death only repeated what she had heard a half hour earlier. This time, however, the time of Claude's return home caught her attention.

Funny, to call it late last night when it was just after nine o'clock, she thought. It wasn't early evening really but it wasn't late either. If they said middle of the evening that would be about right but they probably didn't because it would have an odd sound. Or, her thoughts continued as she went upstairs to get dressed, the news report might be based on some later time when it had been released to the press. Which might not have been for an hour or more after Claude called the police.

Poor Claude. What an awful shock for him. And it had come right after Emily had been so nasty to him on the phone. Not that there was any comparison between the two happenings, but still, it was too bad she had picked a fight, the first real one they'd ever had, just before he had all that horror to face.

She would feel better about it now if only she'd got to the plant in time to catch him on his way out and tell him how sorry she was. But no, that wasn't the way to look at it. It would have made it much worse if she had got there a little earlier; then they would both have had it on their consciences the rest of their lives that if he hadn't stopped to talk to her he might have gone home in time to save Alix. So actually she could be thankful she had missed him at Dunham's and hadn't been able to attract his attention as she followed him home.

A different kind of thought came to her under the shower. Claude was a widower now. After a decent interval, they would be free to see each other openly, giving new depth and perhaps new meaning to their relationship.

She dismissed the thought instantly. How selfish could she get? Here was this great tragedy for all of them, the dead Alix, Claude, and poor wild Julie who would have to face the consequences of what she had done and Emily had to start thinking of how it would affect her.

Instead, she should think of Claude and some way to help him.

But that was no use. There was no way to help him, nothing she could do. She couldn't go near him or even call him to offer her sympathy. She could only wait for him to call her.

"But the stigma of being sent to Central State," Brooke exclaimed with more feeling than logic.

"You think it looks better to be charged with murder and locked up in jail?" Spence inquired.

"You know I don't mean that. But in some ways a mental institution is almost worse."

"That attitude's got cobwebs on it, Brooke. You know it has."

"Even so. It seems all wrong to me. It will hang over her the rest of her life."

"The rest of Julie's life isn't too full of promise anyway," Spence said. "As her attorney, I have to think about what kind of a defense to put up and try to do what's best for her. No question but what the grand jury will indict her for murder when Bruce"—

he was referring to the Commonwealth's Attorney—"presents the evidence."

Brooke looked at him aghast. "But, Spence—she hasn't even appeared in municipal court yet. We don't know yet if—"

"Oh yes, we do. All the law requires is a reasonable amount of evidence for indictment and there's much more than that against Julie. From what I hear, Bruce is real interested in the shots she took at Alix's picture a while back. Makes you wonder if he's got malice aforethought in mind."

"But she was drunk when she did that and dead drunk last night."

Spence shrugged. "Bruce could argue that she was putting on an act that scared Alix so much she called Claude; that she killed her as soon as she hung up the phone and then took a few quick slugs before Claude got home."

"Oh, for heaven's sake, lawyers' talk," Brooke said impatiently but with a worried note underneath.

They were in her living room. It was late afternoon and Spence had stopped by to tell her about Julie's pending committal to the mental hospital.

Brooke got up and walked around the room, turning to look at her brother from the far side of it. "I was with her quite a while last night. She wasn't faking any part of her drunkenness. She was cold, Spence, stone cold."

He didn't answer. He looked tired. It had been a long night and a long day for him, Brooke thought. For all of them, but hardest for him, Julie's lawyer. "We need a drink," she said. "I'll make it."

She left and was back in a few minutes with their

drinks. "What about Dan Graham?" she asked as she sat down.

"He'll arrive first thing in the morning. In time to see Julie before they take her to Central State."

"Will he need a car? He can use mine."

"He'll rent one at the airport."

The house was quiet. Roger's mother had taken the children after school. Roger came in before they finished their drinks. Brooke made him one and said, "Let's all go out to dinner. I don't feel like cooking." She added, "I was just thinking about Julie out in the kitchen. She didn't do it. Drunk or sober."

They looked at each other with raised eyebrows as she continued, "It wasn't in her to do it. I know what I'm talking about. I know her inside out. She'll run wild, get crazy drunk, make big threats but that's it. Look how she took out her feelings toward Alix by shooting her picture. Not Alix herself, although she was right there the whole time. If Julie really wanted to kill her, she was drunk enough to do it then, wasn't she?"

"But Brooke, the evidence against her —" Roger began.

"Purely circumstantial. She didn't do it, she never would have. Whatever real violence there is in Julie has always been turned against herself and never goes all the way to self-murder. No matter what state she's in, she stops short of that." Brooke sighed. "Poor Julie. She can't forgive herself some of the things she's done."

"Well, if we're going to get psychological, wouldn't you say that in one instance at least — the abortion — it's Alix she's never forgiven, calling her baby-killer, putting all the blame on her?" Spence asked.

"That's the point," Brooke replied. "Talk, accusations, all sorts of outrageous things but nothing more. She couldn't kill, not Alix or anyone else. I'm sure of it. I've never been more sure of anything in my life."

Her earnestness had some effect. They valued her opinion.

"Who killed Alix then?" asked Roger.

"That's what we'll have to find out." Brooke finished her drink and handed the glass to Roger, beside her on the sofa. "Be an angel and make me a refill," she said. "Spence too."

When her husband came back with their drinks she resumed: "Motive's a major question in murder, isn't it? Who benefits and all that. The husband is usually the chief suspect when the wife is killed. In books, anyway."

"In real life too," Spence conceded. "Except that in this case, Claude has a good alibi with Uncle Paul to back it up."

"Oh, alibis," said Brooke. "They get broken down regularly in books." In a tone half light, half serious, she added, "But if it isn't the husband, there's always the other woman. Look at Claude. There's been gossip off and on for years about his philandering. To say nothing of the story that was all over town two or three years ago about some girl at Dunham's. Alix got rid of her fast but who's to say there isn't another one now, not so easy to get rid of? After all, Claude's a real handsome man and quite a charmer when he wants to be. We all know women right here in Rockwell who have made a play for him. Alix has had her work cut out for her, keeping an eye on him."

"She always struck me as rather a cold fish," Spence commented. "You, too, Roger?"

"Yes indeed. Not my type. I like 'em plump and cheerful and not at all backward about sticking their noses in other people's business," Roger replied, reaching out a hand to muss his wife's hair.

"You," she said smoothing it down. "You hush your mouth about plumpness or you'll force me to go on a diet and you know how mean I get then."

Spence, ignoring the byplay, said thoughtfully, "He's not seeing anyone around here right now—no one we've heard of, at least."

"Which means none," said Brooke. "If there was a Rockwell woman, we'd hear about it. He goes to Washington a lot, though. Supposed to be business but who's to say no treats on the side?"

"If you start talking about a woman in Washington, you've got to include the suburbs," Roger pointed out. "Plenty of territory."

"Well, if he's been combining business with pleasure, there was some woman up that way connected with that expansion plan he was pushing three or four months ago," Spence said, still only toying with Brooke's theory but on that level giving it thought. "Remember it—the computer thing? Uncle Paul mentioned that Claude had her down to see the plant. She was a young woman, Uncle Paul said, pretty and bright but that cut no ice with him. He was against the plan from the start."

"She's the one," Brooke stated with instant conviction. "A business associate who became a bedfellow."

"Good God," said Roger shaking his head.

192

Brooke paid no attention, warming to her theme. "Maybe Alix got wind of it and there was trouble. Then the woman went to Wayland last night to have a showdown with Alix, wanting her to give up Claude or whatever and walked into this ready-made situation, Julie passed out and the gun in plain sight somewhere. She and Alix got into a fight and the woman just grabbed the gun and shot her."

Brooke paused. "It's a perfectly plausible theory, isn't it?"

"A few objections," Roger said. "For one thing, it would have to be an awful fast fight to build up to a shooting and a getaway in the interval between Alix's call to Claude and his arrival on the scene. And that's assuming that the woman was already on the doorstep when the call was made. Then there's also the matter of—"

"But who's to say the woman wasn't still in the house when Claude got there?" Brooke interrupted. "Don't forget, we only have his version of what he walked in on. He certainly wouldn't give the woman away and let everyone know they were having an affair. Why should he, when he had poor Julie there to take the blame? He'd just tell the woman to get going before he called the police."

Roger and Spence shook their heads in wonderment at the speed with which Brooke had transformed gossamer theory into solid fact.

"She's always had the wildest imagination in the family," Spence said. "Sounds sensible at the start and then—"

"I know," said Roger. "Been coping with it for years now myself keeping us out of lawsuits." He shook his head again. "I'm glad Claude's not around to hear her making him an accessory after the fact."

"You're not so funny," his wife reproved him. "Come to that, how can they be sure—"

"Blood has a habit of drying," Spence said, anticipating her question. "Other indications appear. They're not exact, of course, but the medical examiner puts the time of Alix's death at the earliest moment it could have occurred—which would be immediately after her phone call to Claude."

"All right then, we're back at the woman," said Brooke. "She did it, not Claude."

"But Julie's fingerprint is on the trigger," Roger pointed out. "How do we get around that?"

"She had the gun in her hand. Why shouldn't her fingerprint be on the trigger?"

"It shouldn't be there if this woman you're talking about shot Alix. Her print would overlap Julie's or at least smudge it."

"Oh." Brooke's voice went small but regained its firm note as she replied, "There were three shots fired, Roger. Two hit Alix and one went in the sofa, the last one, probably. How do we know the woman didn't fiddle around after that to reverse the overlapping business and get Julie's print on top of hers?"

"How far out can you get?" said Spence.

"This is too serious for making jokes at my expense," Brooke retorted. "Can either one of you honestly say that the case I'm setting up against this woman—with or without any assistance from Claude—is impossible?"

"No," they said after a moment. "Not impossible."

"Well then, considering that the real impossibility

194

is for Julie to have killed Alix, shouldn't we start looking for proof that she didn't do it, that it was the other woman?"

"How do you plan to go about it?" her brother inquired.

"Well, if it's the woman you mentioned—and let's say it is—Uncle Paul must know her name or something about her. Then we've got to find out all we can about their affair. When and where they meet—"

Brooke's face brightened after a pause for thought. "They'd make phone calls to arrange their meetings, not letters that could fall into the wrong hands. They'd be toll calls, since we're agreed that it's not a Rockwell woman. Phone companies keep back records, don't they?"

"For a certain period," Roger said. "About six months, I think. But Claude would hardly make the calls from home or from his office phone either. A pay phone would be smarter."

He grinned at Spence. "Listen to me. Talking like it's real."

Spence grinned back but they both knew that in spite of themselves they were interested. Brooke could be persuasive.

"Pay phones aren't always convenient," she said next. "I know he wouldn't call from home but wouldn't he feel safe enough at work? There must be a lot of toll calls made at Dunham's, too many to single out his."

"They don't have a WATS line," Spence said. "Uncle Paul's always felt they didn't need one. Now he's beginning to come around."

"Do all calls go through the switchboard?" Roger

asked.

"Most of them. But a few of the top people like Claude and Uncle Paul also have a private phone."

"Does that mean," Brooke inquired, "that each one of the private phones has its own number and the phone company keeps a separate record of toll calls on it, even though they send the bill to Dunham's?"

"I should think so," her brother replied. "I don't see why not."

"How could you find out?"

"Well, I'm sure I couldn't just walk into the phone company and get a look at their records. Police, maybe, under certain circumstances, but not private citizens. They're subpoenaed sometimes too. But in this case—"

"Isn't Tommy Seymour manager of the telephone office here?" Brooke interrupted.

"Now look—" her brother protested.

"He's a good friend of yours, Spence. One of your poker pals, isn't he? He'd let you have an unofficial look. You know he would. As long as it was just for your own private information."

"Lord have mercy, Brooke, if I may quote our late father . . . How do you stand it, Roger?"

"Sometimes I wonder," said his brother-in-law.

"Right away," Brooke said. "First thing tomorrow."

21

Alix's picture appeared Thursday morning on the first page of the suburban section of the morning paper under the headline SISTER ARRESTED IN SOCIALITE'S SLAYING.

The story read: *"Rockwell, Va. Nov. 11. Mrs. Julie Graham, formerly of Greenwich, Conn., was charged yesterday with the murder of her sister, Mrs. Alexandra Whitfield.*

"Mrs. Whitfield, member of a prominent Rockwell family and co-owner of Dunham Office Furniture Co., was found shot to death in her home, Wayland, late Tuesday night by her husband, Claude J. Whitfield.

"Mrs. Graham, the victim's sister, was found unconscious in the same room. She was taken into custody Wednesday morning by Rockwell police and charged with the murder. Pending arraignment in Rockwell Municipal Court, Mrs. Graham will be removed to Central State Hospital, Petersburg, for psychiatric examination."

That was all. Just the bare bones of it, Emily thought, fleshed out a little, but not much, by Claude when he called her yesterday.

He hadn't wanted to talk about it. His voice sounded strained. He said he would call her again when he had the chance but probably wouldn't be able to see her for a few days.

She said that was all right. She said she was very sorry about Alix.

Alix, dead.

Emily studied her picture. Exquisite features, lovely blond hair. A beautiful woman, really, but with an aloof, almost chilly look on her face that wouldn't be to everyone's taste.

Not Claude's, certainly.

What a heartless thought.

What was Claude thinking himself? The good memories he had of their marriage must be shadowed now with guilt and remorse that he hadn't been a faithful husband.

What effect would this have on his feelings toward Emily?

Too soon to think about that yet. There'd be time enough later to sort out whatever damage had been done to their relationship.

Emily went upstairs to get dressed for work.

The day passed. Claude did not call her. She left her office a little earlier than she usually did.

Her doorbell rang soon after she arrived home at five o'clock.

The man standing outside was a stranger to her, a tall man in his late thirties, bareheaded, with thinning brown hair and an average assortment of features redeemed from the ordinary by a thoughtful, slightly quizzical expression. It was Spence Hollis.

"Mrs. Bartlett?" he said.

"Yes."

"I'm Spence Hollis from Rockwell. I'd appreciate it if you could spare me a few minutes."

She stared at him for a moment in stunned silence, feeling as if all the blood in her body had been drained away. Then she stepped aside and said, "Come in, Mr. Hollis."

She led the way into the living room.

"Won't you sit down?" she said, sitting down herself.

Spence sat down and looked at her in open appraisal. Not pretty in the usual sense, although Uncle Paul had called her that. Wedge-shaped face, too narrow in nose and chin. But lovely eyes with brows slightly upslanted. She had got a little color back after turning white as a sheet, a dead giveaway, when he introduced himself.

Even when his gaze shifted to a book on the table, *The Short Stories of Katherine Mansfield*, Emily couldn't give him the same sort of appraisal. She was too frightened by his visit. It meant that he had found out something about her and Claude. The only question was how much. It must be something that had come up since Claude had called her yesterday or he would have told her about it then. Maybe not, though, with all that he had on his mind.

She herself hadn't told him she had tried to catch him at the plant the other night and followed his car home. He had called her at her office and it hadn't seemed the time or place to mention it. She wasn't sure she would ever bring it up. There seemed no point in it now.

Whatever she did about it was in the future. Here in the present was Spencer Hollis, expecting her to ask why he had come—or shouldn't she wait for him to state his business?

Fear wouldn't let her. "Well, Mr. Hollis?" she said.

"I guess you've heard about what happened to Claude Whitfield's wife?" he began.

"Oh yes. Very sad. Very shocking. I never met her although I went to Dunham's one day last summer. Mr. Whitfield showed me around. He had asked me to do a survey—" Emily checked herself. She was saying too much, too fast.

"I know," Spence replied. "I handle some of their legal work."

A lawyer. Her heart sank. What was he here for?

"Do you mind if I take my coat off, Mrs. Bartlett?" He stood up, giving her a fleeting smile.

"Not at all. I should have asked you to." Her heart sank still more. It wasn't to be a short stay.

Spence took off his coat, laid it aside and sat down again.

"Have you been in touch with Claude lately?" he inquired.

It was a trap question, she felt sure, alert to danger, the nature of it not yet clear.

"Well, I'd have to think—"

"No hurry, ma'am." His tone was casual but his eyes had a bright intent look in the lamplight that came from beside him.

Had they been seen together somewhere, Claude and she—or had he let something slip since Alix's death? He couldn't have sent Spencer Hollis here himself, could he?

200

No, of course not. Nothing was less likely than that.

Emily, even more frightened for being all at sea, took refuge in attack. "What is this all about, Mr. Hollis?" she demanded. "You come into my house, a perfect stranger—I think you'd better explain why you came before we continue."

She wasn't going to walk into any trap he set for her, Spence realized. In the first shock of his arrival her face had given away her relationship with Claude. She was in better control of herself now and as bright, apparently, as Uncle Paul had said. But how could a bright young woman have got involved with a man like Claude, a light weight, who'd had one woman or another on the string since he first came to town? There was no answer to that but Spence felt a pang of regret that she had thrown herself away on him.

The next moment he reminded himself of his role of inquisitor. If Brooke was right, Emily Bartlett had more guilt weighting her down than her affair with Claude. Brooke had been right so far. She had even identified the other woman in Claude's life.

"Mr. Hollis," Emily prodded, made more confident by his silence.

Gloves off, thought Spence, and said, "My sister Brooke, who is Julie's oldest friend, insists that she's innocent in Alix's death; that she could never have fired that gun Tuesday night."

"Oh." Emily tried to sound detached. "Has she told the police this?"

"They're conducting their own investigation. We're starting ours from a different point of view." Spence paused. "We felt you might be able to help."

Emily felt a trembling begin inside but kept her voice firm. "I'm sorry but there's no way I can," she said. "I know nothing about it. I can't imagine why you thought I would." She stood up in dismissal. "It's too bad you didn't call me first and I could have told you you'd be wasting your time."

Spence made no move to rise. He went on looking at her with no particular expression on his face. He wasn't ready to leave and even as she got to her feet she wasn't sure that she wanted him to.

"What are you after?" she said.

"I'm trying to find out the truth," he replied. "For everyone's sake, including Alix's. Please sit down, Mrs. Bartlett, and let's see where we get."

Emily sat down slowly. "First of all, you're trying to clear Julie, aren't you? And the way it sounds, at my expense."

"If you mean I'm trying to pin something on you, ma'am, you're quite wrong," Spence said quickly. "Maybe we should start all over again. I don't think I did too well, asking when you were last in touch with Claude. I already know he phoned you twice Tuesday night from his office."

Emily felt as if he had turned a giant spotlight on her affair with Claude, searching out every tender or passionate moment and every mean little excuse or subterfuge that had made them possible. The record kept of toll calls, nothing more than that, had turned this spotlight on her and Claude, reducing their affair to the lowest level of unfaithful husband and willing mistress.

She couldn't speak at first, she felt so scorched

202

with shame under Spence's penetrating but not inimical gaze.

"They were business calls," she managed to say at last.

"Made to your home past eight at night, Mrs. Bartlett? You must have kept on very friendly terms with Claude after your survey was finished. That was quite some time ago."

"We got on well," Emily replied stiffly. "He called the other night to tell me he had some new ideas on his expansion plan."

She looked pointedly at her watch as she said this and got to her feet again. "You'll have to excuse me now, Mr. Hollis. I'm going out this evening and I have some things to do."

"Well then, I mustn't keep you from them." Spence stood up and put on his topcoat.

Emily hurried ahead to let him out but he was more leisurely, lingering in the foyer while she held the door open, her eagerness to see the last of him transparent on her face.

"I hope you'll allow me one more question," he said. "It's just to keep track of everyone concerned. Would you mind telling me where you were, Mrs. Bartlett, from, say, about nine o'clock on?"

"Indeed I would," she retorted sharply. "It's absolutely none of your business!"

He caught an accent of fear as well as anger in her voice. He had learned enough to go on with, he thought, as she shut the door after him. Most important of all, that she had no alibi for Tuesday night.

And yet, somehow, he didn't want her to be the guilty one, he thought, on the way to his car.

Whether she was or not, she would lose no time calling Claude.

But Emily had to lose a little time. She was so shaken by Spence's parting question that she leaned against the door for support.

Not for long, though. She could indulge her fears later after she had called Claude to make sure they told the same story on his two phone calls the other night.

There were just those two calls, it seemed. Claude had always called her from a pay phone until that night. Then, the worst time it could have happened, he had felt so safe from interruption in his office that he had called on his private phone.

Emily dialed the operator and asked for Rockwell Information. But before she was connected, she realized that it would be another traceable call and hung up.

She flung on a coat, picked up pocketbook and keys and hurried out to her car to make the call from an outside phone.

She asked for Claude's number in a drugstore phone booth, dropped coins in the slot and dialed it.

If he wasn't home, she had a message ready to leave. "Miss Murray from Fairfax Distributors," she would say. "Please have Mr. Whitfield call me at his earliest convenience."

He would recognize her maiden name and know it was urgent. But if Spencer Hollis reached him first, it might be too late.

Relief flooded her when Claude answered the phone himself. She began with the same code words. "Miss Murray from Fairfax Distributors."

"Oh yes." A careful note came into his voice.

"I understand you called me twice around eight o'clock Tuesday night, Mr. Whitfield," she continued. "A record was made of the calls. They had something to do with a new approach to your expansion plan, didn't they?"

Oh, my God, Claude thought, what's this about and who's in back of it?

"Yes," he said.

"It might fit in with the Spencer survey," Emily added. "I'd like to talk it over with you as soon as possible."

Spence, checking on his toll calls — what did the nosey bastard suspect?

"Well, let me see . . ." But it was no use thinking about his schedule. He wouldn't have a minute to himself until tomorrow night. He had to go to dinner at Brooke's tonight with Dan Graham. Then Lieutenant Conrad was coming by later in the evening to see Dan and expected Claude to be there too. That took care of tonight and tomorrow was no better. There'd be people around all morning, Alix's private funeral service in the afternoon and the day would be practically over before all the assorted friends and relatives left him in peace.

Tomorrow night was the best he could do and even then, not knowing what was going on, he wouldn't dare go to Emily's for fear of being seen.

"I'll call you sometime tomorrow," he said. "It'll be quite late, I'm afraid, but it's the best I can do."

"You wouldn't have any free time before that even if I arranged to meet you somewhere?" Emily pressed.

Worry was making them less careful than they should be. "I'm sorry, but there's not a chance," he said and then, wanting to end the conversation, "Good night, Miss Murray."

"Good night."

At least she had warned him, Emily thought as she hung up. Spencer Hollis wouldn't catch him unawares.

She put a TV dinner in the oven when she got home and made herself a drink while she waited for it to cook.

She felt too nervous to sit down and went from one room to another with her drink in her hand, halting in front of the terrace door to stare at her image in the glass. But it made her feel vulnerable to the dark outside as if someone was out there watching her. She drew the curtains on it and then all the others on the windows.

She was vulnerable to much more than the dark, she reflected; a charge of murder, Spencer Hollis's questions had implied. She had no alibi to answer him with. She was on the scene in Rockwell, perhaps trying to catch up with Claude at the very moment of Alix's death.

If worst came to worst, would it help to say so?

No indeed. She must never, under any circumstances, admit she had been anywhere near Rockwell Tuesday night. She would just say she was here at home the whole evening and saw no one.

Later, after picking at her uninteresting dinner, she made a cup of instant coffee and took it into the living room. She had started to reread Katherine Mansfield—only Monday night although it seemed much longer ago — and sat down with the book again.

But Spencer Hollis got in the way of reading. She gave it up to review everything he had said from the moment he entered the house until he made his exit with that last chilling question about where she was herself at the time of Alix's death.

He talked about trying to find out the truth but Julie was his sister's oldest friend; their main purpose was to save her and let some outsider take the blame. The whole trend of his conversation made it plain that he considered Emily a likely prospect. It had come out into the open as he left.

But there was something — what was it? — about the way he had worded his last question . . .

It was his asking her where she was from nine o'clock on that night didn't sound right. Shouldn't he have said eight instead of nine? He must know she would have had to leave her house soon after her two phone calls from Claude to reach Wayland in time to kill Alix at nine o'clock. That was when she had died, give or take a few minutes either way.

It was chance, of course, that Spencer Hollis had put it like that, limiting his question to the actual time of the murder.

Funny, though, coming from a lawyer, used to wording questions so as to make their meaning perfectly clear.

Emily frowned in thought and went looking for the suburban section of the morning paper. She read the story on Alix's death again. *"found shot to death in her home, Wayland, late Tuesday night . . ."*

Late last night, the radio report had said yesterday morning. Later reports had said the same thing. She had let it go with the thought that nine o'clock wasn't early in the evening and so they were calling it late.

But now Spencer Hollis had been just as inexact about the time.

Funny . . .

22

Emily spent a wakeful night. Friday morning she went to her office to take care of a few essentials and then left, saying that she wouldn't be back until sometime that afternoon.

By eleven o'clock she was leaving 95 at the Rockwell exit.

She didn't know the town well. It was almost forty miles from Washington, a little too far away to have been engulfed by the suburban tide spreading out from the capital. It still retained aspects of a small Southern city even though large sections of Prince Henry County, which surrounded it, had already succumbed to housing developments and shopping centers.

The highway Emily took followed the river into the business district past the intersecting road she had taken the other night on her way to Dunham's.

This time she stayed on the highway, her first view of Rockwell a tall church steeple rising above the treetops—St. Andrew's Episcopal Church, a gem of colonial architecture, although she didn't know that—then came a mixture of stores and houses as

209

she neared the center of the town, sloping up from the river in a tier of streets.

She passed a row of decaying eighteenth-century townhouses—a project for restoration if Urban Renewal, twelve years under discussion, ever became a reality—and saw a street sign that told her the highway had become Frederick Street. It was the main shopping street, she thought, lined with stores and a variety of business places and presented the usual problem of lack of parking space.

She drove slowly but saw nothing that looked like a library on either side. At the second intersection she came to the traffic light just as it changed to red. She rolled down the window and asked a man on the corner where the public library was.

"Go straight on, ma'am, to the last traffic light three blocks away," he said. "Turn right and you can't miss Courthouse Square. Library's right across from the courthouse."

"Thank you," she said. The light turned green. She followed directions to the last traffic light, turned right and saw Courthouse Square ahead.

It was a quiet backwater with a strip of grass in the middle, centered on a statue, green with verdigris, of some early dignitary of Rockwell, holding a scroll in his hand.

He faced the courthouse. Emily looked the other way and saw the library, Eldred Grant Library, the carving on the lintel said.

Built of some native stone, it seemed small for the size of the town. But then, Emily reflected, as she parked in front of it, it was the fate of libraries to end up at the bottom of most town budgets.

She found herself in front of the desk almost as she crossed the threshold. She asked if the local paper was available, starting with Monday of the present week.

The girl took her around a corner into a small open space that served as the reading room. It was furnished with two tables, a few chairs, and a row of shelves for magazines and newspapers.

"Here you are." The girl placed copies of *The Bulletin* for the past four days in front of Emily as she sat down at a table.

She had the reading room to herself when the girl left. There was no need to cover up where her real interest lay by pretending to look at Monday or Tuesday's paper. She laid them aside.

A much larger version of Alix's picture, the one she had already seen, was prominently displayed on the front page of Wednesday's issue. The big black headline over it read DUNHAM HEIRESS SLAIN; SISTER CHARGED.

The story gave much more background detail than Washington papers had carried. Emily skimmed through it until she came to the end of the column. The last sentence read, *"Police estimate that the fatal shooting occurred around 9:45 p.m. in the interval between Mrs. Whitfield's telephone call to her husband and his arrival home shortly before ten o'clock. (See Slaying, col. 1, page 3)."*

Emily read it twice, three times. How could they have got it so wrong when it should say nine, not ten o'clock?

Nearly an hour wrong . . .

But even as she thought this, news and radio

reports ran through her head; late last night; late Tuesday night. There was Spencer Hollis's question too . . .

Could some local reporter, first on the scene, have got the time wrong and then all the news media repeated his mistake?

Something like that must have happened, Emily told herself. But her hands shook turning to page three.

There was no further mention of the time the shooting took place.

There was no mention of it in Thursday's paper either, except for the familiar phrase, late Tuesday night. The story said that the police investigation, under the direction of Lieutenant William Conrad, was continuing; that Julie had been taken to Central State Hospital; that Alix would be buried in the family lot in St. Andrew's Cemetery Friday afternoon with the Reverend Lucian Wood, Rector, conducting the private funeral service.

Emily put the newspapers back on the shelf and left, stopping at the desk to thank the girl for her assistance.

She went out to her car but made no move to start the motor, sitting back instead and lighting a cigarette. She wasn't keeping her usual count of how many she had smoked today. She had too much else on her mind. She had to find an explanation of the discrepancy in the time of Alix's death that would take away the cold weight inside her; a better one than a reporter's mistake.

There was one, of course. Presently it came to her. Claude could have made two trips between Wayland and his office Tuesday night. When she saw him at nine o'clock he could have been on his way home to get something he needed at work and then have gone right back to Dunham's. There would have been time enough, just about, for him to have got settled down at his desk again before Alix's phone call.

He might even had a little margin left over, the way he was driving when Emily saw him Tuesday night; too fast for her to catch up with him at all. So fast, in fact, that when she heard about Alix's death the next morning she had wondered if an emergency call from her might have been the reason for it. She hadn't stopped to think that he always drove fast.

Two trips must be the answer. Or else the newspapers had got the time wrong, unlikely as it seemed.

The best way to find out was to call the police. They would have a record of what time Claude called them.

She had noticed a phone booth at the corner where she had turned toward Courthouse Square. Stop there to make the call, she thought, before she got too nervous to make it at all.

She looked up the number and dialed it.

"City Police, Hadley speaking," a voice said.

"Is Lieutenant Conrad there?" she asked.

"Lieutenant Conrad? Not right now, ma'am. Would you care to leave a message?"

"Is there anyone else I could talk to about the Whitfield case?"

"I'll connect you with Sergeant Rhodes."

"Sergeant Rhodes," the next voice said.

"I'd like to know what time Mrs. Whitfield's death was reported to the police Tuesday night," Emily said.

"Can you give me that information, sir?"

It was a matter of public record but the sergeant hesitated. "Who's calling, please?"

Katherine Mansfield was the first name that came into Emily's head. "Mrs. Mansfield," she replied. "Mrs. Kitty Mansfield of 3981 Glebe Road, Arlington."

"The call was logged at 9:58 P.M., ma'am. May I ask why—?"

"Thank you." Emily hung up.

She went back to her car. No more question of a newspaper mistake. She was left with her other explanation. Claude had made two trips.

There was no reason why he should have mentioned it when he called her Wednesday; and certainly not during their brief cryptic conversation last night.

When only one explanation made sense it had to be accepted.

And yet there was still that cold weight inside her. It wouldn't go away until she saw Claude.

Sergeant Rhodes shook his head when Emily hung up on him. Nut call, he thought. A major crime stirred up the nuts. At least this one hadn't tried to give him some worthless tip that would waste the department's time.

He dismissed it from his mind—or thought he did—until he went out a little later to have a quick lunch at the coffee shop across the street.

Spence Hollis was there ahead of him sitting at the counter. They had gone to high school together. The sergeant sat down on the next stool and said, "How's

214

tricks?"

As they talked a little about the murder, noncommittal talk, considering the different roles they played in it, Sergeant Rhodes thought of Emily's call. It was a safe topic to bring up and one that would evoke sympathy for the long-suffering police department.

"These nuts," he said at the end.

Not a nut, thought Spence. Not at all. Mrs. Kitty Mansfield—that book on the table yesterday—was Emily Bartlett.

But it was an odd sort of call for her to make, he thought on his way back to his office. Whether she had killed Alix herself or not, why should she be so interested in what time the murder was reported to the police?

He had to put the question away until Alix's funeral was over. Attendance was limited to relatives and close friends, and these were not invited to Wayland afterward as they would have been under different circumstances. Brooke had offered to have them at her house instead and went around after the graveside service telling everyone to come by.

Sandwiches and drinks had been prepared but the usual relaxed atmosphere that followed a funeral, reminiscences of the deceased, ancedotes that brought laughter and a reaffirmation of life, were missing. It was a constrained gathering with Claude Whitfield, the chief mourner, the most silent of all.

He could hardly wait for it to be over. He would still have Dan Graham staying at Wayland but at least not on his hands this evening. Dan had accepted Paul Dunham's invitation to dinner while Claude declined it, intending to be on his way to see Emily as soon as

Edna went home.

He had to stay at the Parkers' until the group broke up. But he left with Dan Graham right after the last guest was gone. He had kept his distance from Spence Hollis all afternoon.

Nobody could object to his wanting to be alone tonight, he thought. If Dan got back to Wayland ahead of him that was all right too. He would say he hadn't felt like going to bed and had gone out for a drive. He would let nothing keep him from seeing Emily. He had to find out what Spence Hollis was up to. He wouldn't have an easy moment until he did.

Claude would have been more frantic than uneasy if he could have heard the conversation Spence had with Brooke and Roger after his departure. He took them into Roger's den out of earshot of the maid tidying up the living room and told them about Emily's call to Sergeant Rhodes.

"What bothers me is why it should matter to her what time Alix's murder was reported to the police," he said. "Especially if she killed her. The smartest thing for her to do in any case was stay out of it entirely."

"Of course she killed her," said Brooke. "The choice lies between Julie and her, doesn't it? And I'm more convinced than ever that it wasn't Julie after what Dan told me she said yesterday."

"What was that?" asked Spence.

"She said that in a funny sort of way Alix's death had freed her of a lot of things she was carrying around from the past; that for the first time she felt as if there was some hope of straightening herself out in the future; and that she knew, deep inside her, that

216

she'd never have such feelings if she'd killed Alix herself."

"Feelings, honey, are no substitute for proof," Roger said gently.

"They're good enough for me," Brooke replied. "And since I know Julie is innocent, I also know Emily Bartlett must be guilty."

"There's Claude," her brother said, as surprised as they were that he said it.

"But look at his alibi, Spence," Brooke pointed out. "He was at his office — Uncle Paul called him —"

"No," said Spence. "He called first and had Uncle Paul call him back. Makes you wonder . . ." He paused and then picked up on a new tack. "Mrs. Bartlett will probably shut the door in my face but I'll try to see her again soon." He didn't add that he rather wanted to.

"Give her time to cool off first," Roger advised.

While they were discussing Claude and Emily another conversation that had to do with them went on at the police station between Lieutenant Conrad and Sergeant Rhodes.

It had started with a call from Arthur Jones. He had been out of town yesterday, he said and, hadn't seen the Washington papers. His receptionist, however, had recognized Alix's picture and saved it for him. He called to tell Conrad about Alix's visit to him and then added his own impression that what she really wanted to find out was if the unnamed businesswoman she mentioned was going out with her husband.

They speculated that the woman Alix was interested in might be the one who had called Rhodes that morning. The Arlington police reported that no Mrs. Kitty Mansfield lived at the address given.

But it was all very tenuous. Jones's impression — he seemed pretty sharp, though, Conrad interjected — and Alix's suspicion, never checked out.

They had Julie Graham cold for the murder with no question in their minds of having charged the wrong person until Jones's call came in.

"She was served up to us on a platter," Conrad remarked without pleasure.

"By Whitfield himself," Rhodes said.

Experienced police officers, they were suddenly sharing qualms about their too-perfect case.

"Wouldn't hurt to take a good look at Whitfield," said Conrad.

"Reckon we should," Rhodes agreed.

23

Claude was out of the house immediately after Edna left that night and called Emily from the nearest pay phone.

"Where shall we meet?" he asked. "Not at your place. The visitor you had yesterday puts me off."

Emily thought for a moment. "Remember the restaurant where we had dinner last week and you said the peanut butter soup and country ham were so good?"

No one could be listening in, there was no reason for her to avoid naming the Alexandria restaurant they had gone to, but jumpy as she was, caution governed her every word. "How about meeting in the cocktail lounge there?"

"Fine." There were booths, he recalled, and it was seldom crowded. "I'm still in Rockwell, though, so you'll have to allow me about three-quarters of an hour to get there."

Emily, with a much shorter drive, had leeway to change from a suit into a dress and renew her make-up so as to look well for Claude who would clear up all the fears that had plagued her since her trip to

Rockwell that morning.

She was the first to arrive at their meeting place and secured a booth at the far end of the dimly lighted room. The dining room was busier than the cocktail lounge at that hour, going on eight o'clock.

As Emily sat down, she remembered that she'd had no dinner herself. She had worked late and was just starting to get it ready when Claude called her. She ordered a sandwich with her drink when the waiter said he could serve her one there.

It had just been placed in front of her when Claude came in the door, glanced around and saw her.

He was wearing a dark suit. He looked tired, his face thinner in just these few days, she thought, as he walked the length of the room to her far corner.

"Darling, it's so good to see you." He kissed her and sat down. When he saw her sandwich he added solicitously, "But why didn't you order dinner if you haven't eaten yet?"

"They wouldn't serve it out here. This is all I want, anyway. How about you—have you eaten yourself?"

"Oh yes. I was home alone—Dan Graham went over to Paul's—and Edna gave me an early dinner a little after six."

"How are you?"

"Well . . ." He shrugged.

The waiter appeared. Claude ordered bourbon and water. He tried to keep his tone matter-of-fact as he asked how everything was with her. He would have to let her finish her sandwich before he brought up Spence's visit. A man with nothing to fear wouldn't show too much concern over it.

He mentioned how heavy the Friday night traffic

was on 95 and went on to other small talk that took them through half of the sandwich, Emily too nervous to eat the rest of it or contribute more than a word or two herself.

Presently Claude said that he might go over to the plant tomorrow, that there was a lot to be straightened out and that he expected to be very busy for the next few weeks.

Emily nodded. It didn't occur to her that he meant to convey the message that she must not make too many demands on his time just because Alix no longer stood in their way. He saw that the message was wasted but there would be other ways to get it across later. He was a free man now. A rich man, too, inheriting Alix's share of Dunham's and her half-interest in Wayland, through the joint will they had made years ago.

If she had lived a little longer, she would have changed it.

She hadn't though. Which made him a free man, a rich man who needn't tie himself down again in a hurry. He could have his cake and eat it too with Emily while he was supposed to be in mourning and at the same time look the field over . . .

"Something else?" he inquired when Emily had eaten as much as she could of the sandwich.

"No, thank you."

He gave her a cigarette, lit one himself and leaned back in the booth. "Tell me about Spence," he said.

"He hasn't mentioned that he came to see me?"

"Not a word."

"So I needn't have taken the chance, calling to warn you last night."

221

"Well, at least I get to see you." Claude's smile hid his impatience.

Emily gave him an almost verbatim account of what had been said, deeply branded as it all was in her mind.

Claude let his face register the right expressions, regret that he had made traceable calls to her, outrage that Spence should suspect her of the murder.

"Although I'd put nothing past him or Brooke, trying to save Julie," he said, signaling the waiter to bring them another drink. "You did all you could, telling him they were business calls."

"But he didn't believe me," Emily said when the waiter had come and gone. "Not for a minute. Not at night to my home number. Even so"—she looked at Claude steadily—"they hardly seem enough by themselves to have brought him to my door so fast."

"Well, Paul met you last summer. Spence or Brooke could have checked with him and put a few things together." He could hardly add, "Including a few other episodes in my past."

After a moment he said, "I can't tell you, darling, how much I regret that you've been brought into this. Makes me mad just to think of the nerve Spence had. If he ever shows up again, don't let him in. He can't even prove how close we've been to each other, to say nothing of trying to pin Alix's death on you."

Claude meant to reassure himself as well as Emily. Let Spence sniff around like a hound dog on the scent for all the good it would do him. Plenty of men had affairs with other women without their wives getting killed over them, didn't they?

"We'll see . . ." Emily's voice trailed off. Now she

222

would have to ask Claude about Tuesday night. But why was she tied up in knots over it? He would explain it all in a few words—two trips to the plant—and then she could relax and forget the worries that had hung over her all day long.

She took a swallow of her drink. "How's Julie?" she began in as good an opening as she could think of.

He was abrupt in his reply, Julie the last person he wanted to talk about. Still at Central State, he said, her arraignment coming up in Municipal Court sometime next week, her husband staying on for it.

"I've been wondering," Emily continued, weighing each word, "how long it was after you called me that night before Alix called you about Julie."

"Quite a while." Claude frowned slightly, this being another subject he didn't want to discuss.

"Well, how long was that?" Emily persisted.

"It was sometime after nine-thirty. But look—"

"Oh, you worked that late? When you called me at eight o'clock, you didn't expect to be there as late as that."

"Well, when you wouldn't meet me, it didn't matter how late I worked, did it? So I stayed right there at my desk until Alix called me. And now, if you don't mind"—his tone sharpened—"let's talk about something else. It's not like you, Emily, to keep probing at a sore spot."

"No, it isn't. But in this case I have to. Because—" Her voice failed her. Her heart beat so fast that she had to stop to get her breath. "I went to Dunham's that night, Claude. I wanted to tell you how sorry I was over the way I'd acted on the phone. You were just leaving when I got there—you cut in front of another car and it honked at you—I honked, too, trying to get your attention but you just kept going—"

Her gaze was fastened on his face. Claude couldn't meet it. He fought for control. But this was a blow that caught him totally unprepared, a thunderbolt that came from out of nowhere. His own heart pounded. He missed a little of what Emily said as he tried to bring order to his whirling thoughts.

"—couldn't catch up with you at all," she went on haltingly. "I was still quite far behind when you turned in at Wayland. I looked at my watch. It was five after nine—" Her voice faltered into silence. She looked down at her glass, turning it around and around on the table, not wanting, not able to think yet of why he had lied to her about Tuesday night.

Claude wiped sweat off his face and said, "Emily . . ." Then as she looked at him he found himself not ready to begin and beckoned the waiter.

Emily had barely touched the drink in front of her and shook her head when Claude suggested she have another with him. All she wanted to do was get up and leave. But she couldn't do that. He had a right to be heard.

When the waiter took his order and left he made a fresh start. "I'm ashamed to tell you how stupid I was the other night," he said. "I couldn't believe it when I walked into the house and found Alix dead—it must have just happened because she was still bleeding a little—and Julie passed out in a chair. You can't imagine how stunned I was, Emily. I remember yelling at Julie to wake up and then rushing out of the room. I drew a blank after that . . .

"Next thing I remember was pouring myself a drink. When I looked at my watch it was almost ten o'clock. I'd been home nearly an hour. I didn't know what to say to the police after waiting so long to call them. I didn't want to tell them the truth. I was too ashamed of the way I'd panicked. Any man would be, I can assure you, although a woman might not mind so much. Then, as I thought it over, what had happened seemed so obvious that I couldn't see what difference it would make if I said Alix didn't call me until after nine-thirty. So that's what I did and from then on I was stuck with the story . . ."

Emily's tension eased a little as she listened. The waiter came with Claude's drink. He made some remark and Claude answered it.

It gave her a further respite. She leaned back in the booth.

What Claude had just told her could well be true, given the kind of person he was. She had known all along, hadn't she, that he wasn't the smartest man in the world? There was the inept way he had handled that plan for expansion; the way he had exaggerated his own importance at Dunham's—lied about it, actually—and then come running to her like a hurt child when Alix cut the ground from under him. She had guessed at other lies since in some of the things he said about his job.

It was his habit, in other words, to boost his self-esteem with lies whenever it seemed necessary. It might well be that he had found it easier to lie to the police the other night than to admit that he had blanked out for the best part of an hour through sheer panic.

The folly of lying in anything as serious as a murder case need not have occurred to him until later — didn't childish behavior often include avoiding immediate embarrassment without regard for future consequences? — and by the time Claude realized what a great mistake he had made, it was too late to change his story.

He'd had reason to look appalled when she said she had seen him the other night. No one would want to be caught in such a lie as that. She couldn't tell him that he had just made her realize he would always lie under stress.

It destroyed all respect for him. But you could still, she reflected, care about not hurting someone's feelings even though respect was gone.

In acceptance of this, Emily reached across the table and laid her hand over his.

She believed him. Claude felt a surge of relief and triumph. "Oh Emily, honey —" He gave her a quick smile and gripped her hand tight. "You don't know what it means to tell you the truth and have you understand."

Her answering smile was as maternal as her hand pat. "My drink's just melted ice," she said. "Will you order me another and then we'll both go home. You must be tired. So am I. I didn't sleep well last night and I have a nine o'clock appointment at the office tomorrow morning."

"Tomorrow? It's Saturday."

"Yes, but occasionally there are people who can't make weekday appointments. I've got one of them coming in tomorrow. It will be a three- or four-hour session and then, I suppose, the salesman and I will take the man to lunch. So you see, I need some sleep."

Claude finished his drink in one gulp and ordered another for each of them, shrugging off her reminder that he had to drive home when they left.

"I'm fine," he said. "Strong head for liquor."

Wooden head for everything else, she thought.

They kissed good night in the restaurant parking lot. Emily drove away depressed by the thought that everything was changed between them. Claude didn't know it yet; he assumed that they were back on their old footing. They never would be, though, after his inglorious behavior the other night. But at least the doubts and fears that had haunted her all day were gone.

Claude sat in his car after she left, making no move to leave himself. He felt drained by Emily's revelation, the last thing he would have dreamed of. He had worried, of course, over what Spence had found out about their affair, but on the big issue, Alix's murder, he had begun to feel safe.

Safe. Jesus, he was sitting on a powder keg. Emily could blow him sky high at a moment's notice. A word to Spence, a word to anyone—

What were her thoughts on her way home? She had believed his story, a right good one, considering the circumstances, but would she go on believing it when she had time to think it over?

No way of telling. It didn't matter, over the long run, whether she did or not. Maybe the run was no longer than the hearing in municipal court next week. He had no idea how much would be brought out then or how much of it would get in the newspapers. If that alibi he'd fixed up—not worth much, anyway, if his phone setup was ever questioned—got into print and Emily saw it, his goose was cooked.

He groaned aloud. If only he hadn't been so goddamned clever he'd be home free. Even if Emily began to doubt his story, she wouldn't go to the police without proof that it was a lie. Once she had it, that was the end. She'd do her duty, regardless of what came out about her affair with him. And sooner or later, at the hearing or at Julie's trial, that proof would be dumped in her lap.

If only he'd stayed off the phone to Paul the other night. If only—

Never mind that. Now he had to think of what to do about Emily.

Sweet Christ, he had to do something . . . And there was no time to lose.

24

Emily got home from her Saturday appointment in midafternoon. The rest of the day and a long quiet Sunday stretched ahead, allowing too much time to wonder what was happening in Rockwell in the light of what Claude had told her last night. There was her own new attitude toward him to supplement this cheerless train of thought.

From now on she would look for ways to break off with him. It would have to be gradual—she didn't want to hurt him if she could help it—but their relationship was at an end.

It would make it easier, she thought, that they should stay away from each other, right now, anyway. When he called her, she would keep putting him off or, at the most, meet him somewhere for a drink or dinner. She would have many pangs over what she was doing, she would miss him at first, but she would never let him come to her house again.

He wasn't to know that, of course. She would handle it so carefully that when he looked back on it later he would think of it as something that had just happened to them, a drifting apart.

In the meantime, though, she had to keep it to herself that they had come to the parting of the ways . . .

Emily wished presently that she had brought some work home from the office to take up her time. She could read or watch TV tonight but she would need something to keep her busy tomorrow.

A phone call a little later gave her spirits a small lift. It was a friend in Bethesda, Maryland, inviting her to Sunday dinner. Just a few people, she said, to meet a college classmate of her husband's who had arrived unexpectedly yesterday.

Emily laughed when an apology was made for the short notice. "I'm not proud," she said. "I'm pleased to be invited. What time?"

"Oh, since it's Sunday, a little earlier than usual. Drinks around five, I guess. Can you make it then?"

"That's fine with me," Emily replied. "I'll look forward to it."

It would at least get her out of the house, she thought, as she hung up. It made tomorrow look less bleak.

The evening paper came. Before she sat down to read it, she took a veal cutlet out of the freezer to thaw and then fixed herself a drink. Watching the six o'clock news took up more time. The phone rang in the middle of it but as soon as she answered whoever had called hung up. Wrong number, she thought, going back to her chair.

The day was passing. It was time to start dinner when the news was over.

She scrubbed a potato and put it in the oven to bake. Too soon to make a salad but she might as well bread the cutlet.

The box of bread crumbs was on a high shelf of the cupboard next to the sink. Emily stood on tiptoe to reach it instead of getting the stool. The box slipped out of her hand. She made a wild grab for it to keep bread crumbs from spilling all over and knocked her kitchen radio, plugged in near the cupboard, into the sink. It struck the faucet with a crackling flash of blue light. The kitchen lights went out. She had blown a fuse.

"Well, that's a funny one," she said aloud and went out into the hall to turn on a light there. When it didn't come on she realized that it must be on the same circuit as the kitchen lights.

The panel of circuit breakers was in the outside wall near the stairs. The wall light part way up the stairs reached the panel but she got out a flashlight for a better look, studying the chart to see what each circuit breaker controlled. She found the one marked KITCHEN-HALL when she tried to reset the switch nothing happened.

She went back into the kitchen but only looked at the radio hesitating to touch it.

The maintenance man lived around the corner in one of the apartment buildings. Emily looked up his number and called him. Knowing she always tipped for extras, he said he would come right over.

He arrived a few minutes later. He got out his own flashlight—she had never seen him when he wasn't carrying it, along with various tools in his back pockets—and looked at the radio.

"Well, you didn't unplug it, ma'am," he said reproachfully reaching for the cord. "Of course you can't reset the circuit breaker while it's still plugged in."

He unplugged the radio, ambled up the hall to the panel and reset the switch. Lights came on.

"See?" he said, leathery face crinkling with satisfaction as he returned to the kitchen. "Nothing to it, ma'am, once you unplugged the radio."

"It scared me stiff," Emily confessed. "I was afraid to touch it. I can't imagine"—a puzzled note came into her voice—"why it did that. It's just an old thing I've had for years but it's never acted up like that before."

"Want me to take a look?" The maintenance man reached into his pocket for a screwdriver, removed the back and peered inside.

"Hmmm," he said after a moment as much to himself as to her. "What's that wire doing—? Shouldn't be there—"

What wire?" Emily tried to see over his shoulder.

"That one." He tapped it with the screwdriver. "It's the power cord, ma'am, but what's it doing connected to the volume control? Lord have mercy, old radio like this, metal knobs and all, you could have been electrocuted when you turned it on. Had it in a repair place lately?"

"No," she said in a faint voice.

"Then I don't see how it could have got hooked up this way."

But Emily, with blinding suddenness, saw.

The maintenance man tinkered with it for a few minutes, screwed the back on it again and straightened up. "There," he said. "It's okay now." He turned it on, got a blare of music and nodded approval as he

232

turned it off.

"All set, you see." He put away his flashlight and screwdriver. "But I still don't understand," he added perplexedly, "how it could have happened."

"I must have knocked against it, jostled it some way—" Emily hurried to get her pocketbook, took out two dollars and handed it to him.

"Thank you very much," she said.

"But I still don't understand it, ma'am. No matter what kind of rough treatment you gave it." He was still shaking his head as he left.

Emily made her way slowly to the living room and sat down.

Could have been electrocuted—could have been electrocuted—electrocuted—

The words took on a terrible rhythm of their own marching through her head.

Old radios. Metal knobs. Power cord connected to the volume control switch.

The maintenance man might not understand how it could have happened but she understood with ice-cold certainty.

Claude had rigged it up with intent to murder her.

As he had murdered Alix. And she had swallowed his story whole last night, distressed over it but in the end, condescending in her belief that he had been inadequate in a crisis.

And all the while, there was somewhere a piece of evidence in wait that would tell her, when she found out about it, that every word he said to her last night was a lie.

He had only been buying time with that story of his while he worked out a way to kill her. It had to look like an accident. He couldn't risk two murders in the same week.

Emily groped unseeingly for a cigarette. Old radio. Maybe some repair shop messed it up, they would say. Even if there was suspicion over her death, there was nothing to connect it with Claude.

And she had thought him inept.

She huddled deeper in the chair shivering until her teeth chattered.

A drink would help, a straight shot. She spilled some pouring it.

Claude. Just this afternoon she had been thinking of being careful not to hurt him when she broke off their relationship.

God in heaven, what a fatuous fool she had been. Ready to accept any reasonable explanation last night as she told him about following him home.

No wonder he'd had that appalled look on his face. How his mind must have reeled when he'd thought he was so safe.

Emily started shivering again. Another drink, smaller this time.

Oh God. She had slept with him, enjoyed his company, admired his looks, thrilled to his lovemaking.

He was a skillful lover—practiced.

Oh God.

Echoes of her own voice. She was fond of her old radio she had told him once. Turned it on more than TV actually.

She had told him last night that she would be at her office this morning. It had given him a clear field to come into her house using the spare key she had left out for him one night last month when she thought she would be late.

He still had it. He kept forgetting to return it.

He had a key to her house. She got up on the instant to put the chain on the door and check the lock on the terrace door. Then she went from room to room drawing the curtains tight.

Was Claude out there in the dark waiting? Or had he seen the maintenance man arrive and known he had failed?

Failed to electrocute her—how could it be true?

It was true. It was to cover up Alix's murder.

But she couldn't just sit there with her mind going around in circles. She had to do something. She had to tell the police.

The phone rang, a commonplace occurrence suddenly frightening.

She answered it, her hand tentative on the receiver as if it might turn into a lethal weapon or convey some new horror.

Which it did through a listening silence on the other end. Claude, checking to find out if she had been electrocuted yet—as he had earlier when she'd thought it was a wrong number.

"Don't hang up again, Claude," she said sharply. "I know why you're calling."

A quick-drawn breath and then his voice protesting, "But, honey, you hardly gave me a chance to speak. What's the matter? You sound real worked up over something."

"I am. It's not every day I just miss being electrocuted."

"What? Why, Emily—"

"Don't bother pretending it's news to you," she said. "I don't know where you are—maybe just outside my door watching. But if you are you're wasting your time. The police are due any minute."

She hung up, aware that the conversation was a mistake. He hadn't given her a chance. Or Alix. Or for that matter, Julie. But now she had given him one. A chance to run, try to get away if he could.

She lifted the receiver and dialed the operator.

"This is an emergency call," she said. "Please get me the Rockwell police."

SPINE TINGLING HORROR
from Zebra Books

CHILD'S PLAY   (1719, $3.50)
by Andrew Neiderman
From the day the foster children arrived, they looked up to Alex. But soon they began to act like him—right down to the icy sarcasm, terrifying smiles and evil gleams in their eyes. Oh yes, they'd do anything to please Alex.

THE DOLL   (1788, $3.50)
by Josh Webster
When Gretchen cradled the doll in her arms, it told her things—secret, evil things that her sister Mary could never know about. For it hated Mary just as she did. And it knew how to get back at Mary . . . forever.

DEW CLAWS   (1808, $3.50)
by Stephen Gresham
The memories Jonathan had of his Uncle and three brothers being sucked into the fetid mud of the Night Horse Swamp were starting to fade . . . only to return again. It had taken everything he loved. And now it had come back—for him.

TOYS IN THE ATTIC   (1862, $3.95)
by Daniel Ransom
Brian's best friend Davey had disappeared and already his clothes and comic books had vanished—as if Davey never existed. Somebody was playing a deadly game—and now it was Brian's turn . . .

THE ALCHEMIST   (1865, $3.95)
by Les Whitten
Of course, it was only a hobby. No harm in that. The small alchemical furnace in the basement could hardly invite suspicion. After all, Martin was a quiet, government worker with a dead-end desk job. . . . Or was he?

Available wherever paperbacks are sold, or order direct from the Publisher. Send cover price plus 50¢ per copy for mailing and handling to Zebra Books, Dept. 2079, 475 Park Avenue South, New York, N.Y. 10016. Residents of New York, New Jersey and Pennsylvania must include sales tax. DO NOT SEND CASH.